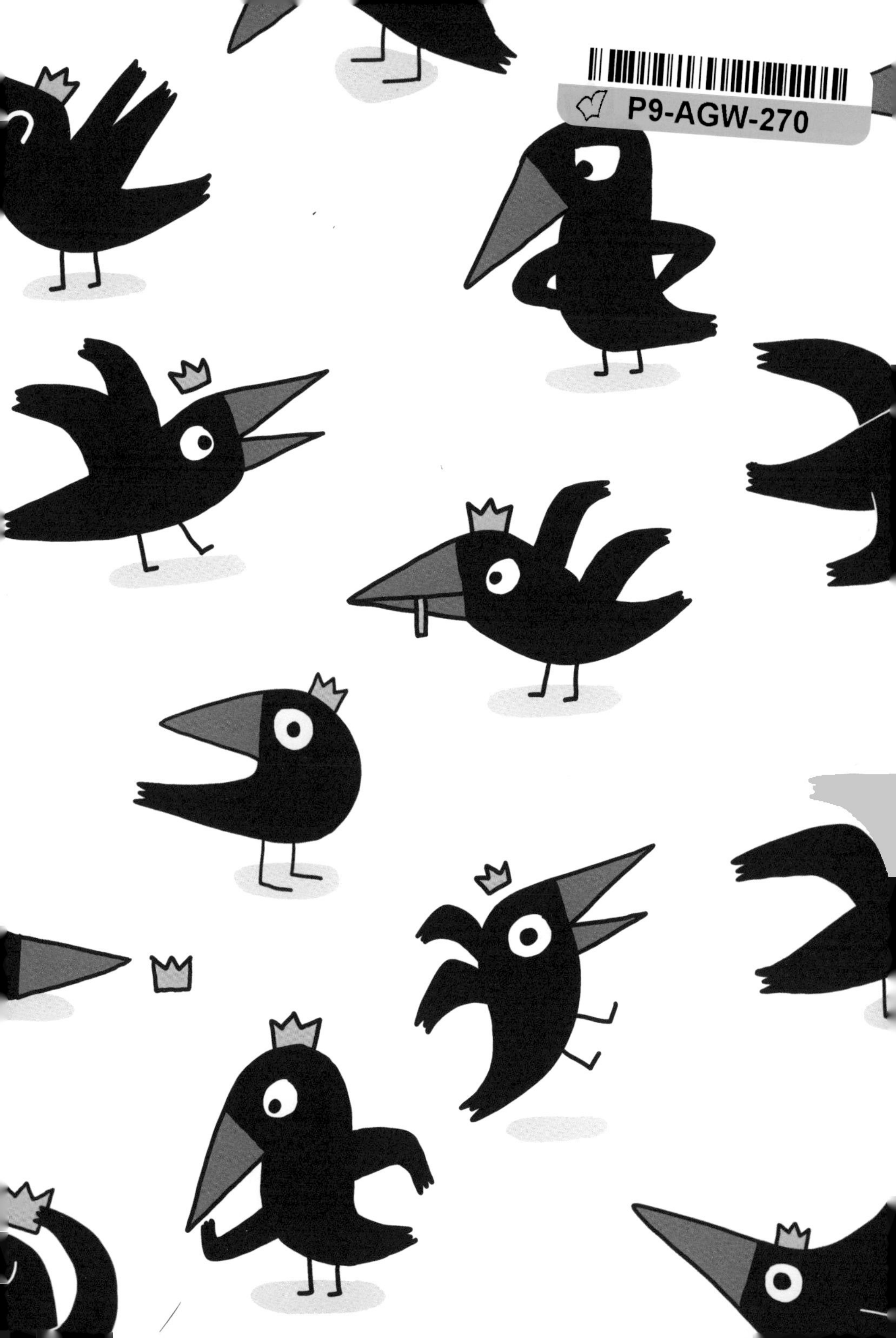

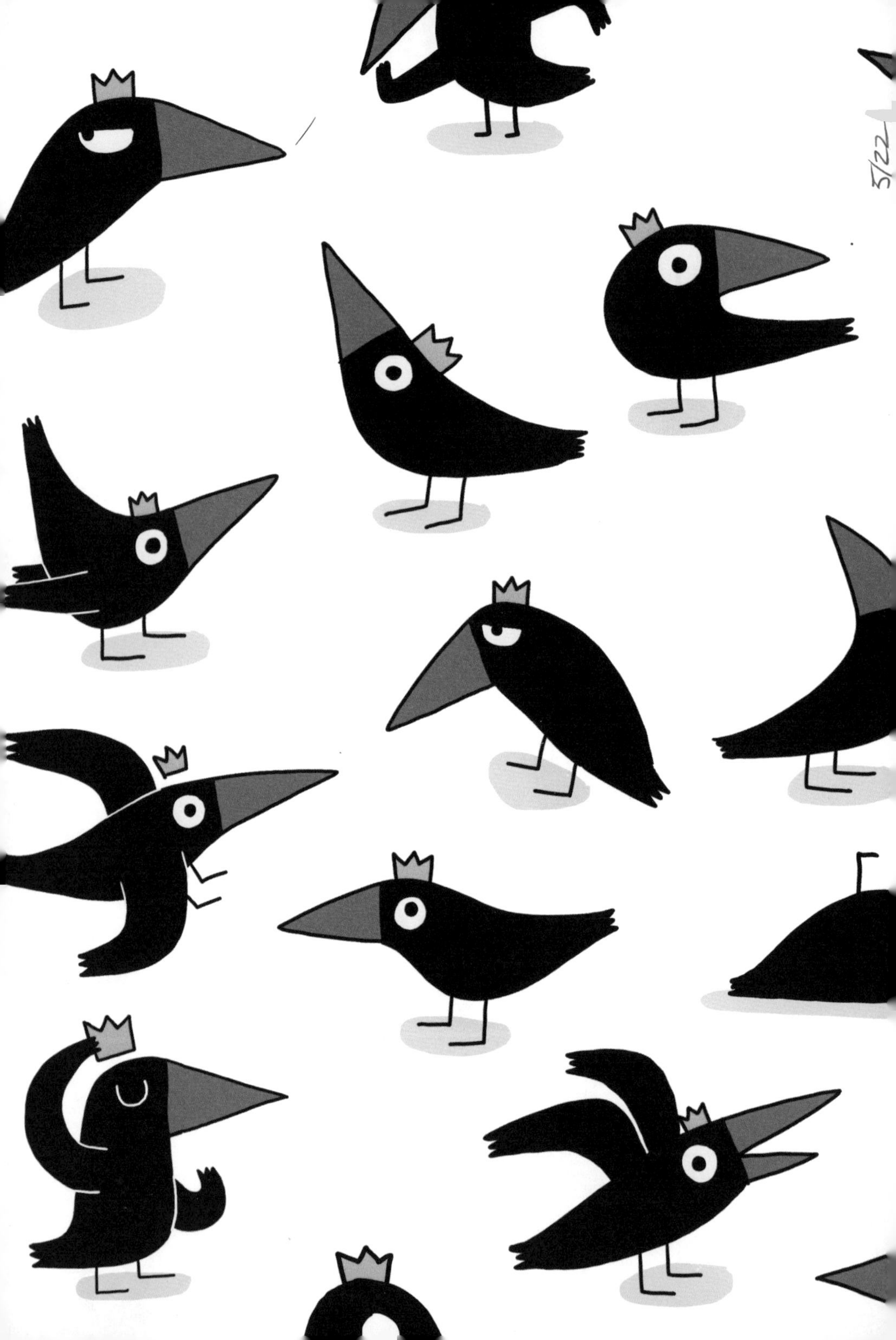

☆☆☆ ARLO & PIPS ☆☆☆

NEW KIDS IN THE FLOCK

ELISE GRAVEL

HARPER alley

An Imprint of HarperCollins Publishers

HarperAlley is an imprint of HarperCollins Publishers.

Arlo & Pips #3: New Kids in the Flock
Copyright © 2022 by Elise Gravel
All rights reserved. Manufactured in Bosnia and Herzegovina.
No part of this book may be used or reproduced in any manner whatsoever without written permission except
in the case of brief quotations embodied in critical articles and reviews. For information address HarperCollins
Children's Books, a division of HarperCollins Publishers, 195 Broadway, New York, NY 10007.

www.harperalley.com

Library of Congress Control Number 2021948115
ISBN 978-0-06-235125-8 (trade bdg.) — 978-0-06-305079-2 (pbk.)

The artist used Photoshop to create the digital illustrations for this book.

21 22 23 24 25   GPS   10 9 8 7 6 5 4 3 2 1
❖
First Edition

For Enzo,
who is almost an Arlo

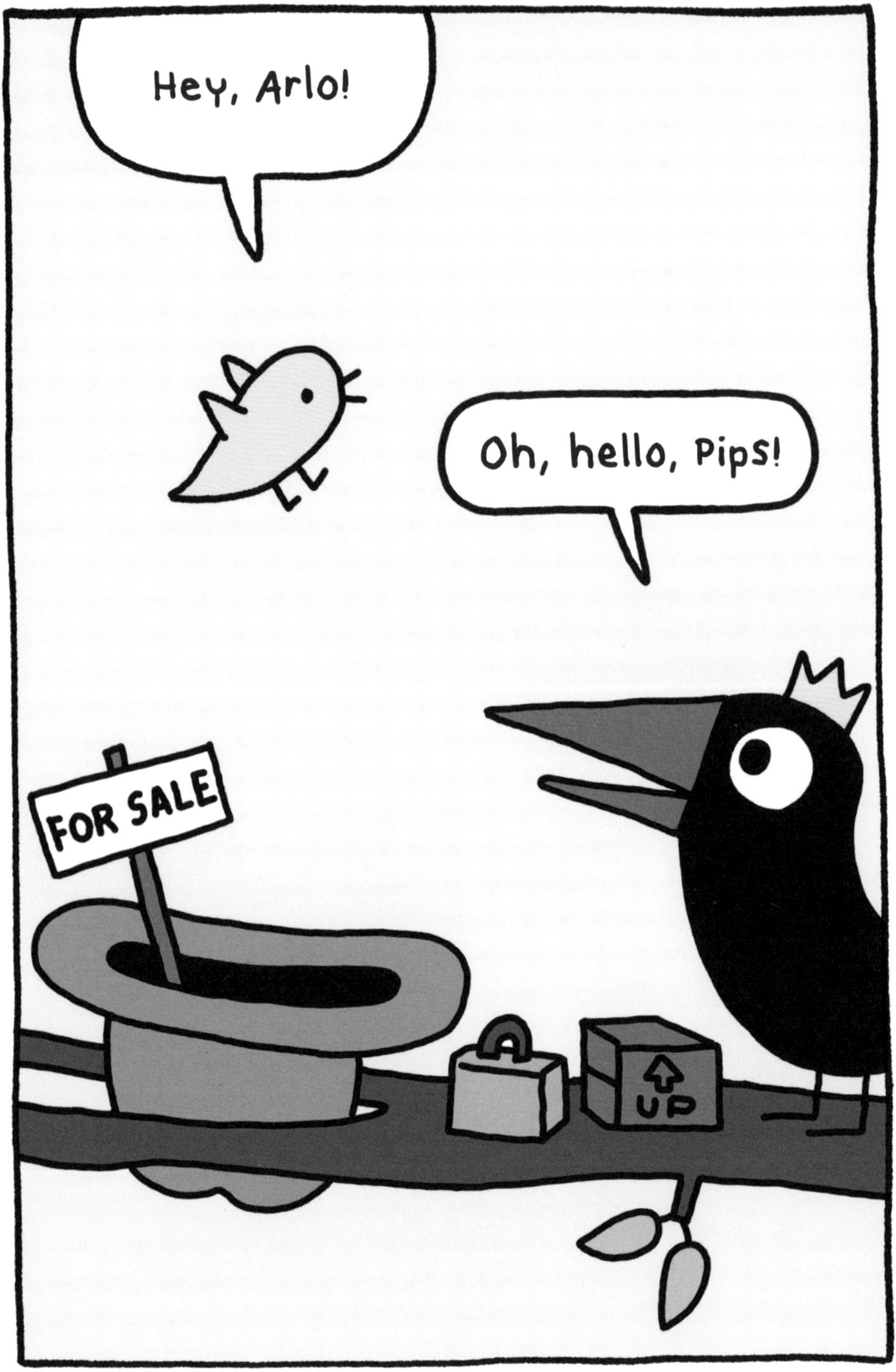
Hey, Arlo!
Oh, hello, Pips!
FOR SALE
UP

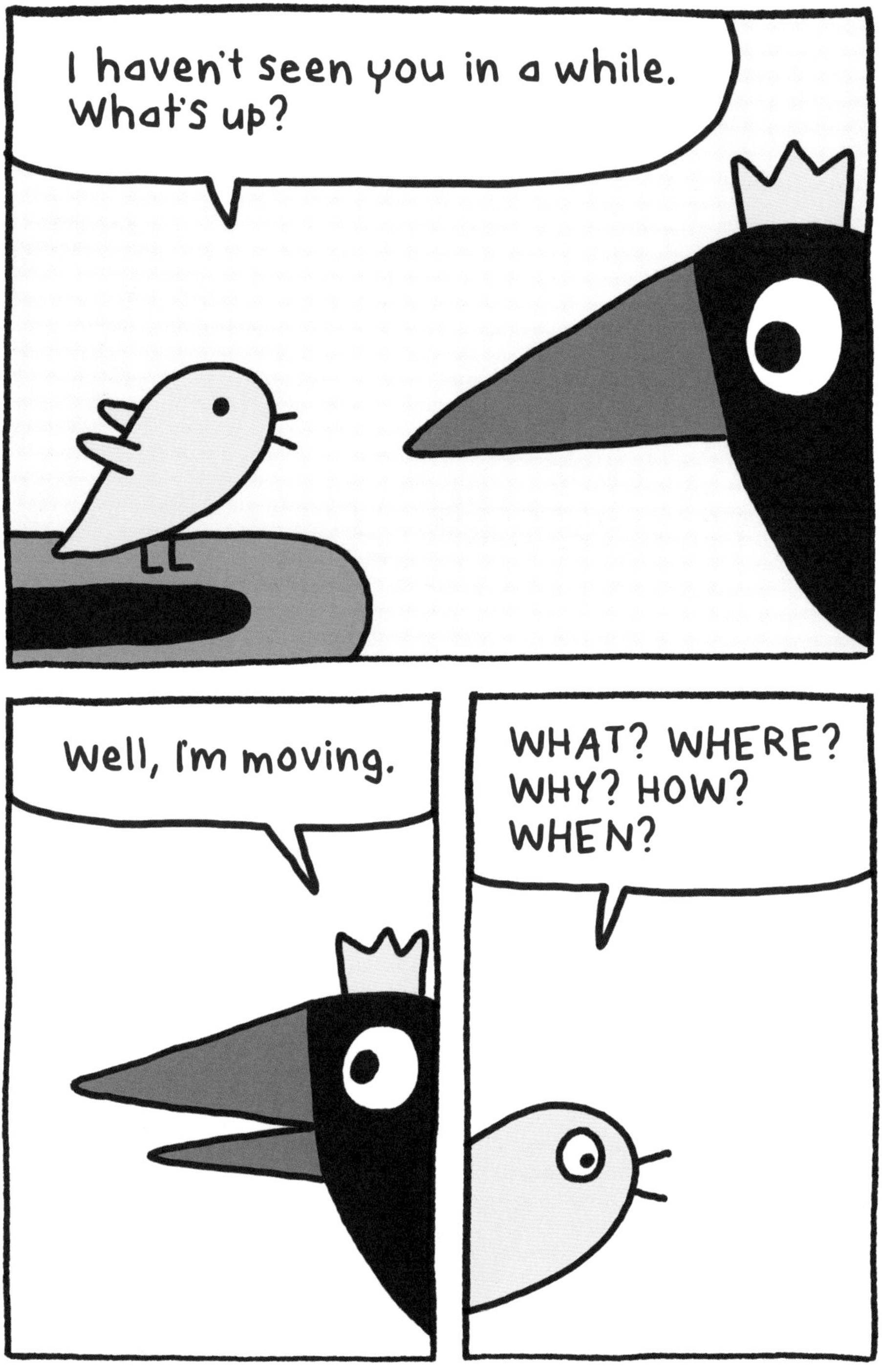
I haven't seen you in a while. What's up?
Well, I'm moving.
WHAT? WHERE? WHY? HOW? WHEN?

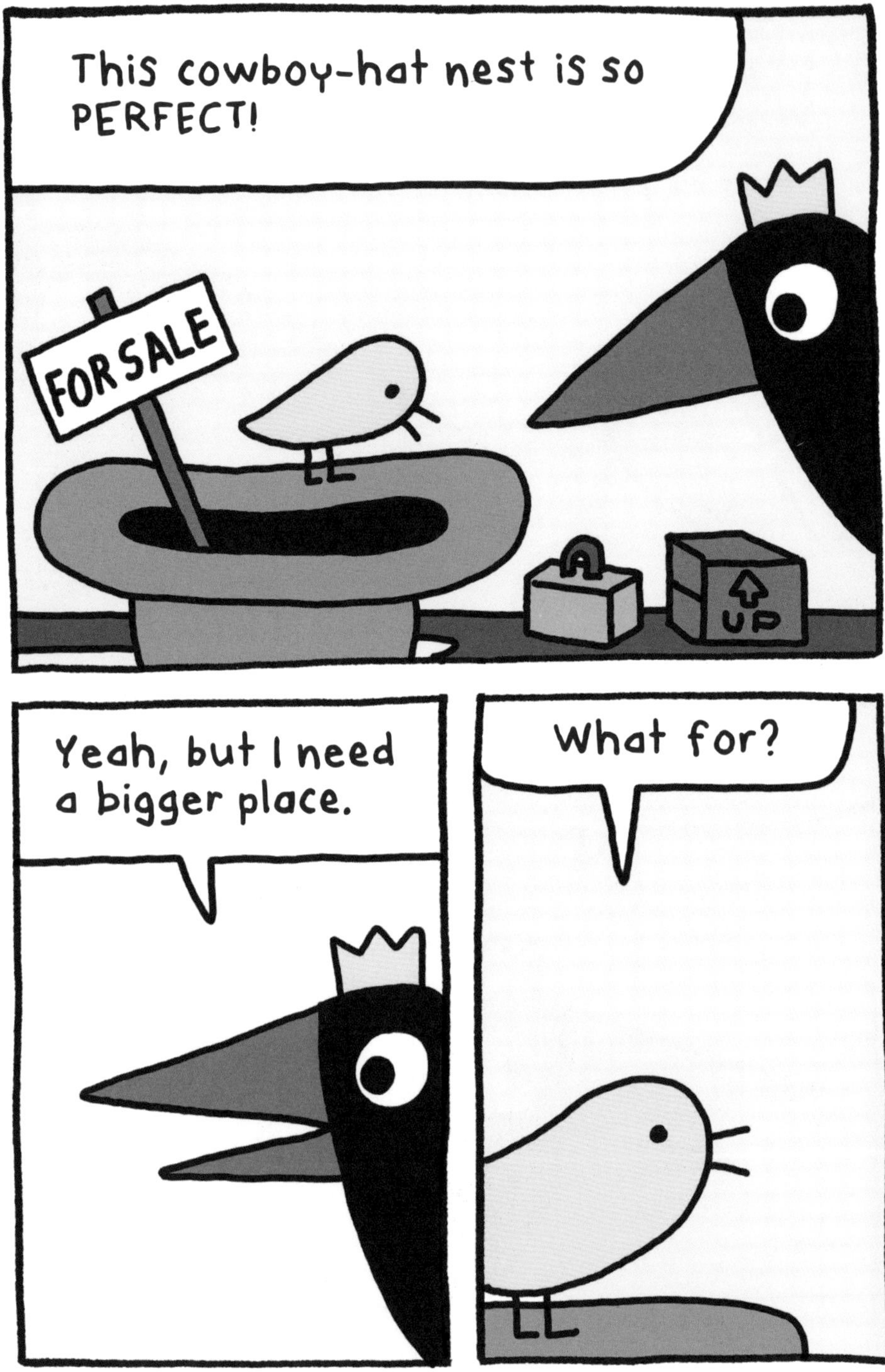
This cowboy-hat nest is so PERFECT!
FOR SALE
UP
Yeah, but I need a bigger place.
What for?

To put all the toys.
Toys?
What toys?
The kids' toys.
The plushies,
the balls, the
building blocks...
I don't understand.
What kids?

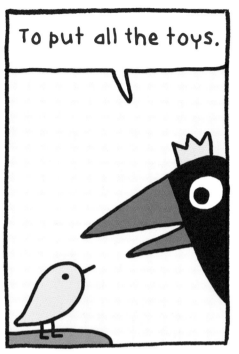

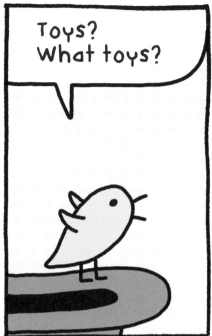

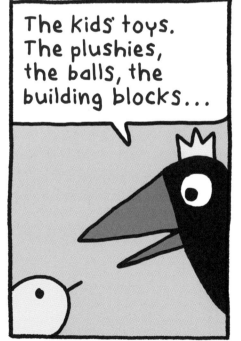

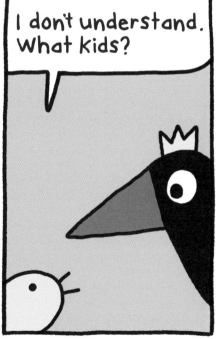

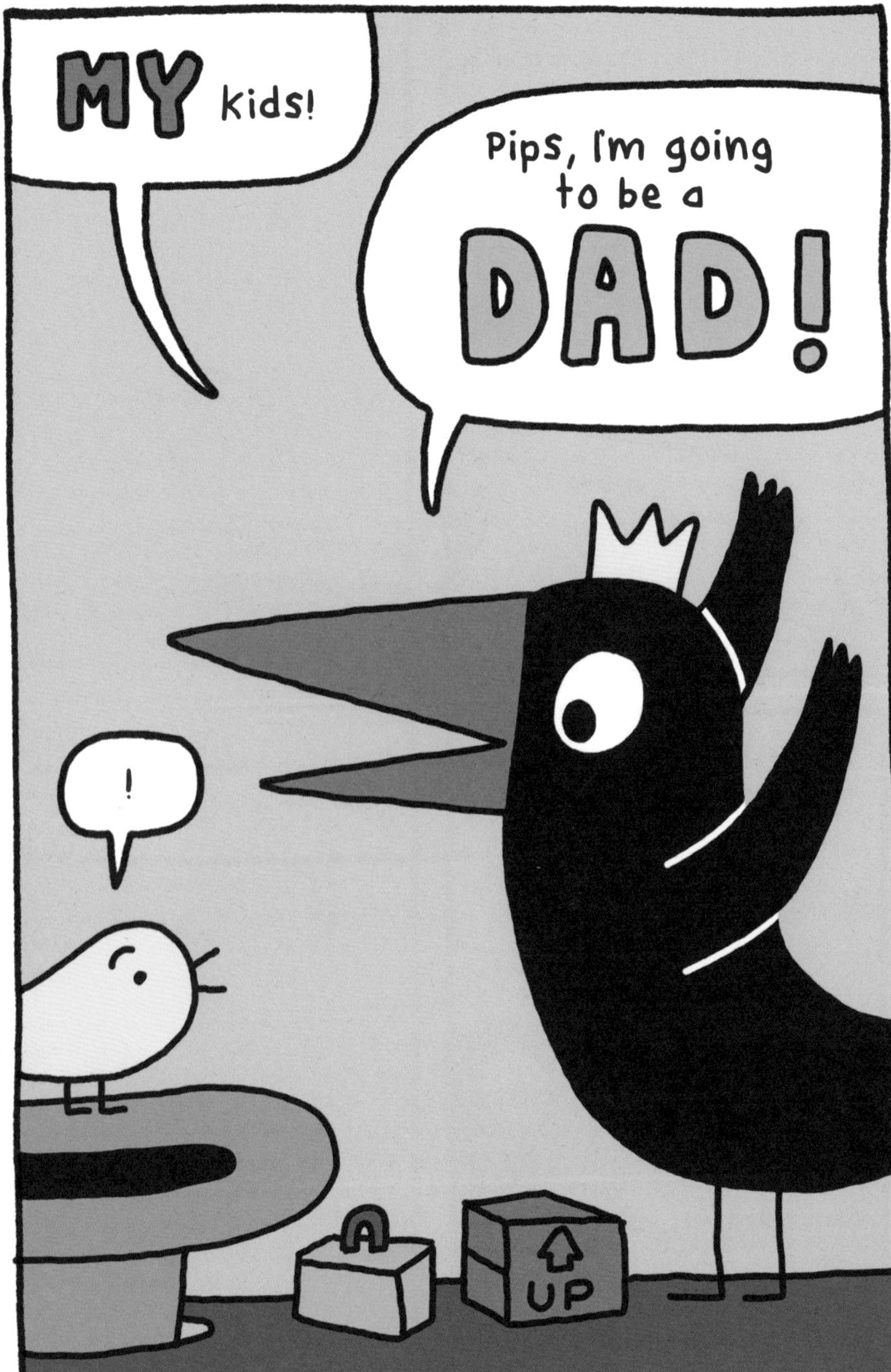
MY kids!
Pips, I'm going to be a DAD!
!
UP

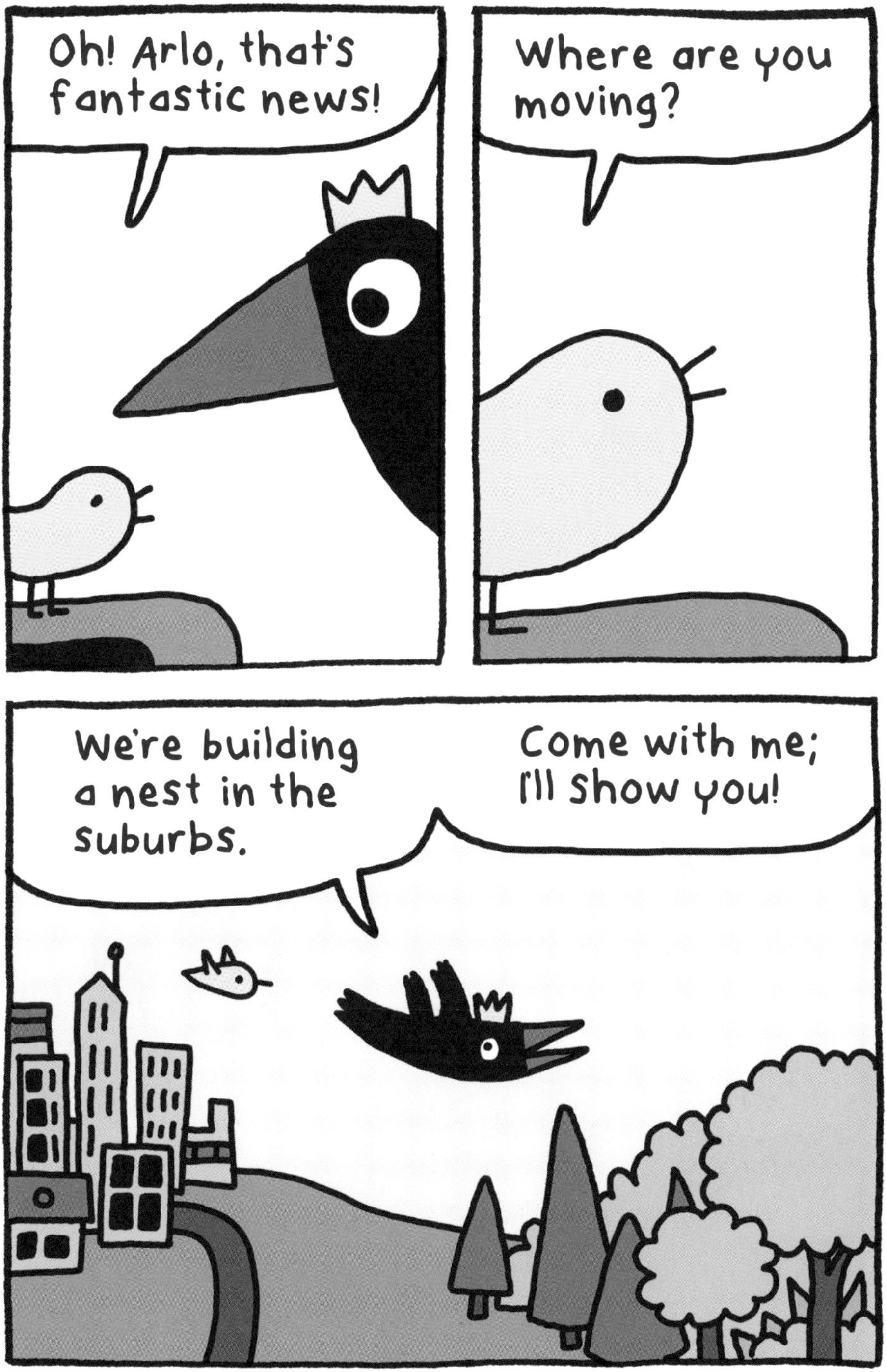
Oh! Arlo, that's fantastic news!
Where are you moving?
We're building a nest in the suburbs.
Come with me; I'll show you!

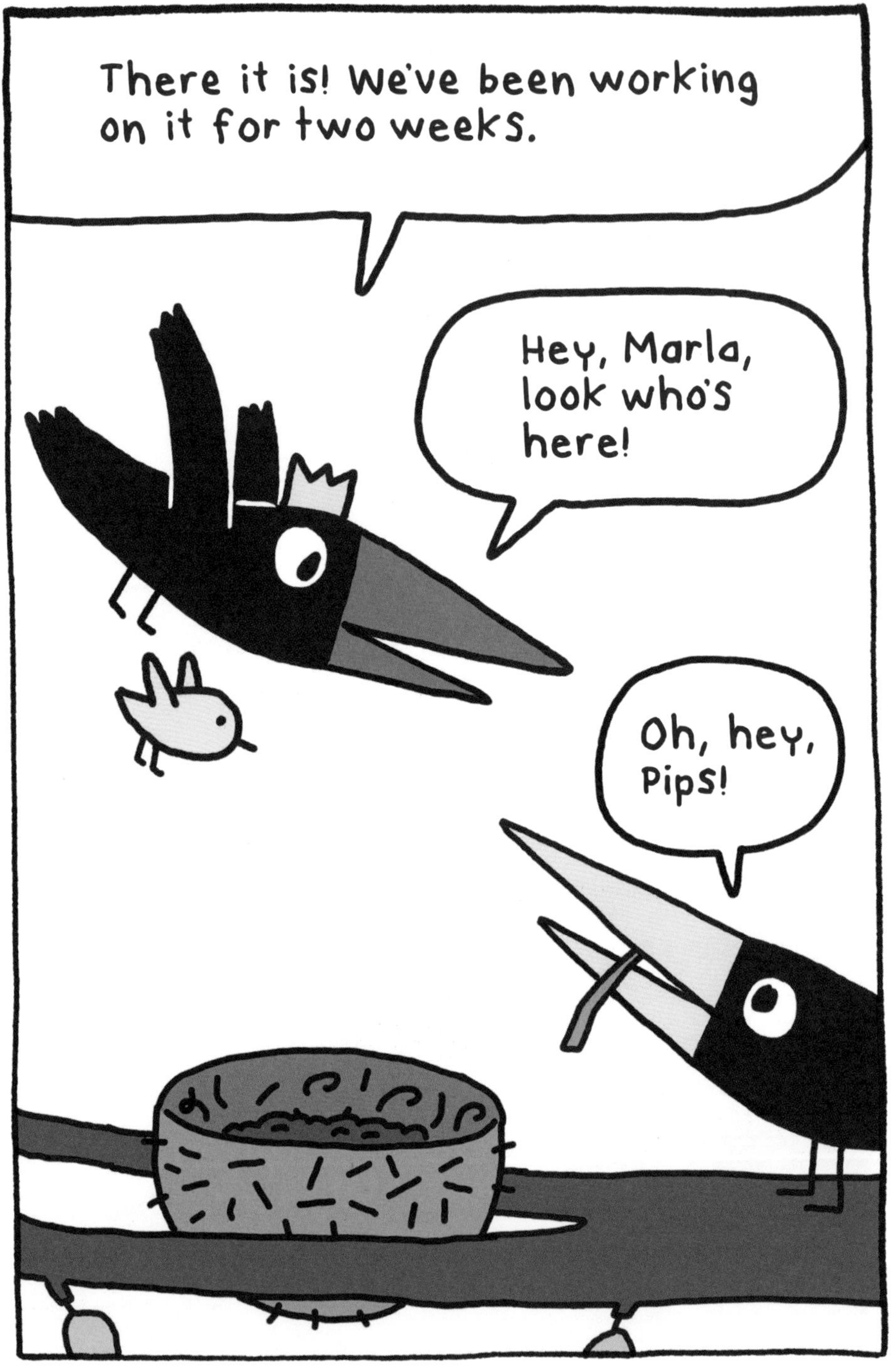
There it is! We've been working on it for two weeks.
Hey, Marla, look who's here!
Oh, hey, Pips!

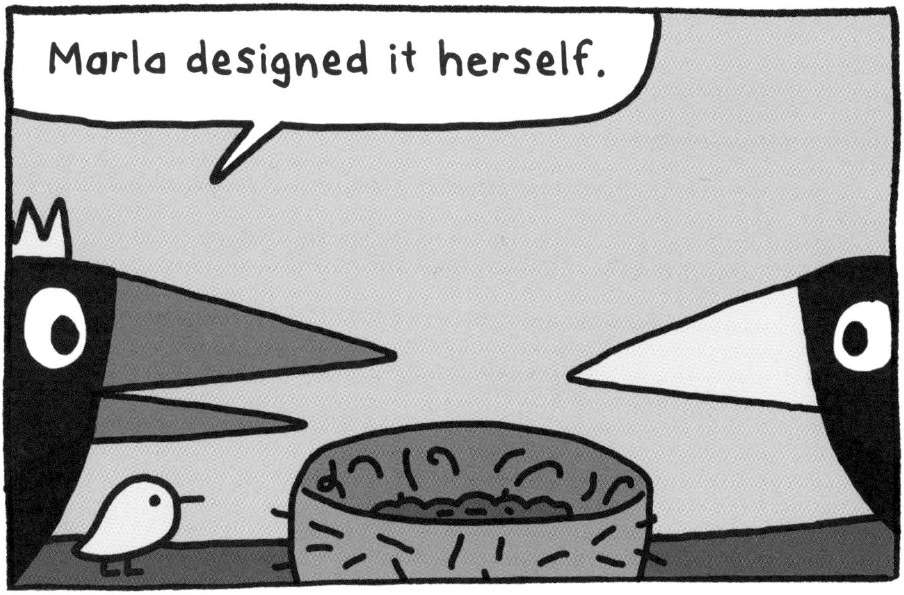
Marla designed it herself.

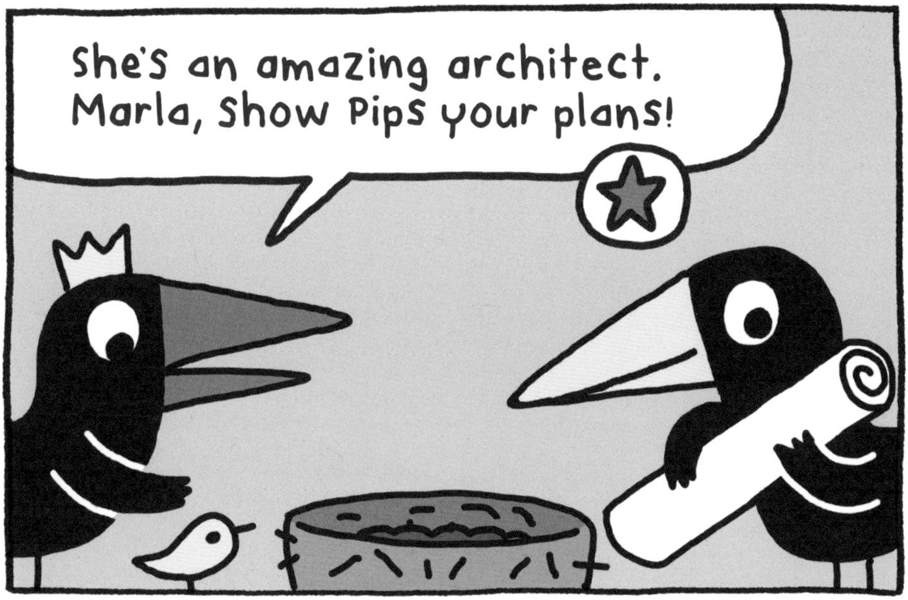
She's an amazing architect.
Marla, show Pips your plans!

★ Crows carefully design their nests and take up to two weeks to build them.

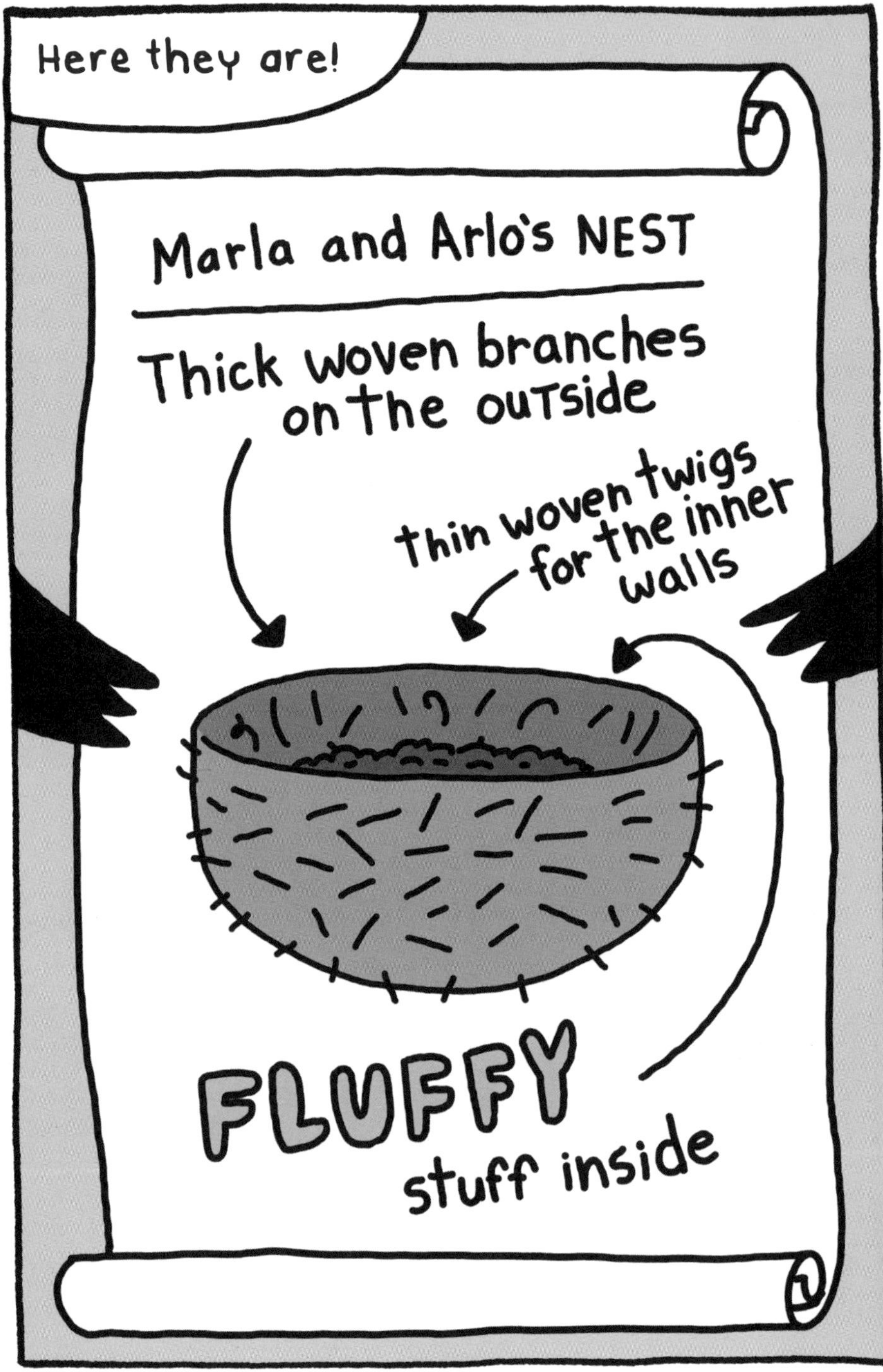
Here they are!
Marla and Arlo's NEST
Thick woven branches on the outside
thin woven twigs for the inner walls
FLUFFY stuff inside

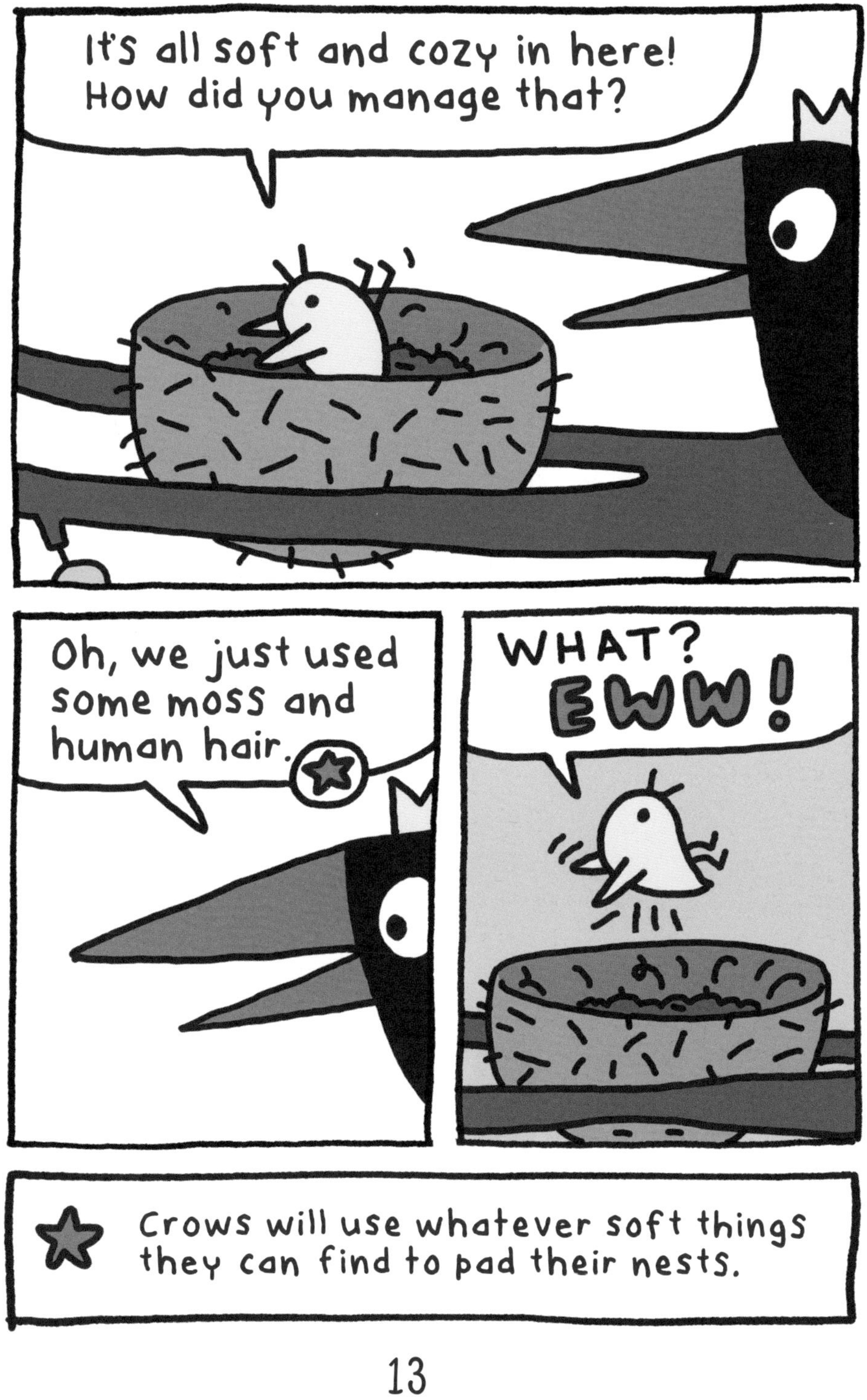
It's all soft and cozy in here! How did you manage that?
Oh, we just used some moss and human hair.
WHAT? EWW!

Crows will use whatever soft things they can find to pad their nests.

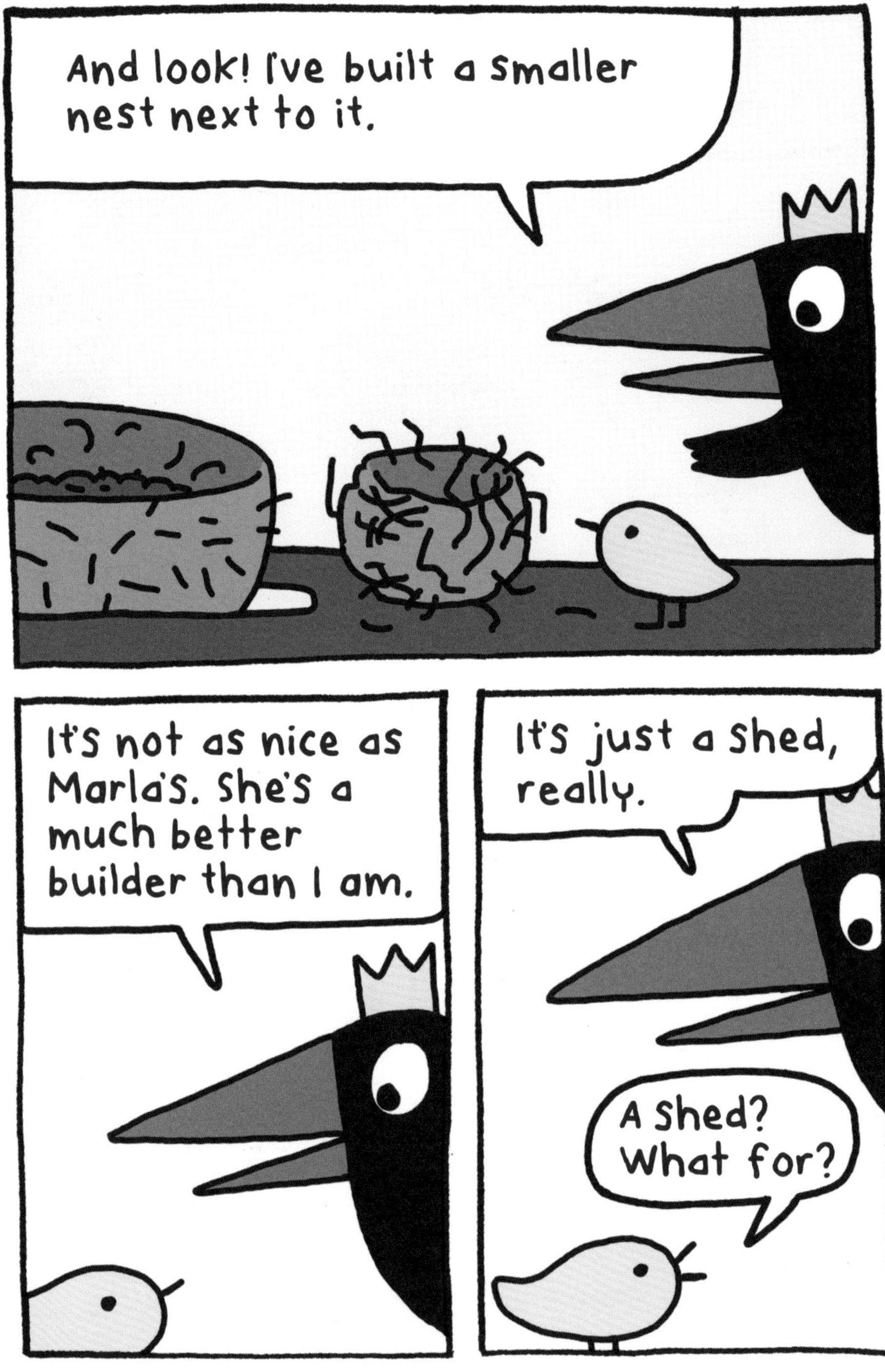
And look! I've built a smaller nest next to it.
It's not as nice as Marla's. She's a much better builder than I am.
It's just a shed, really.
A shed? What for?

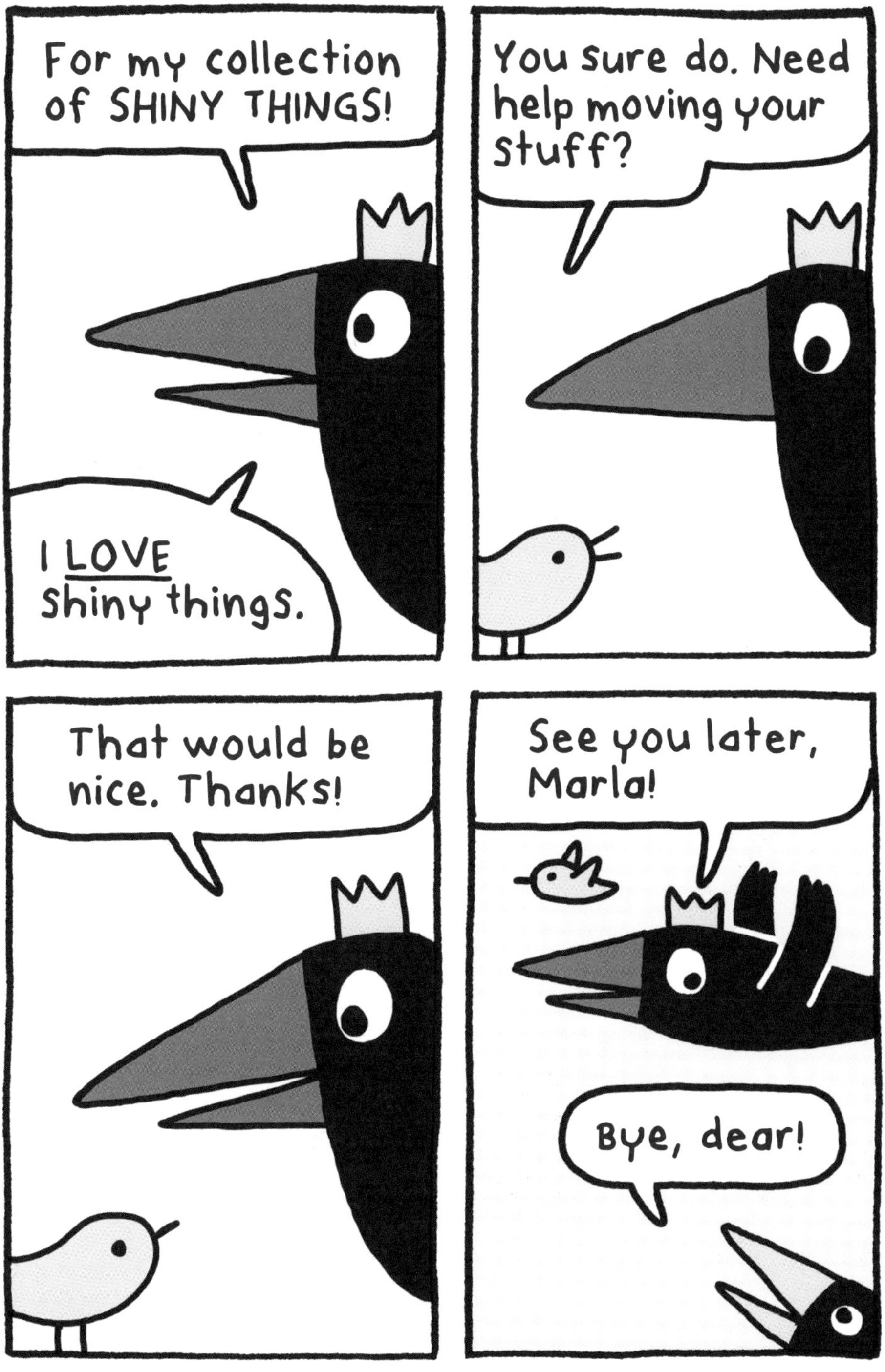
For my collection of SHINY THINGS!
I LOVE shiny things.
You sure do. Need help moving your stuff?
That would be nice. Thanks!
See you later, Marla!
Bye, dear!

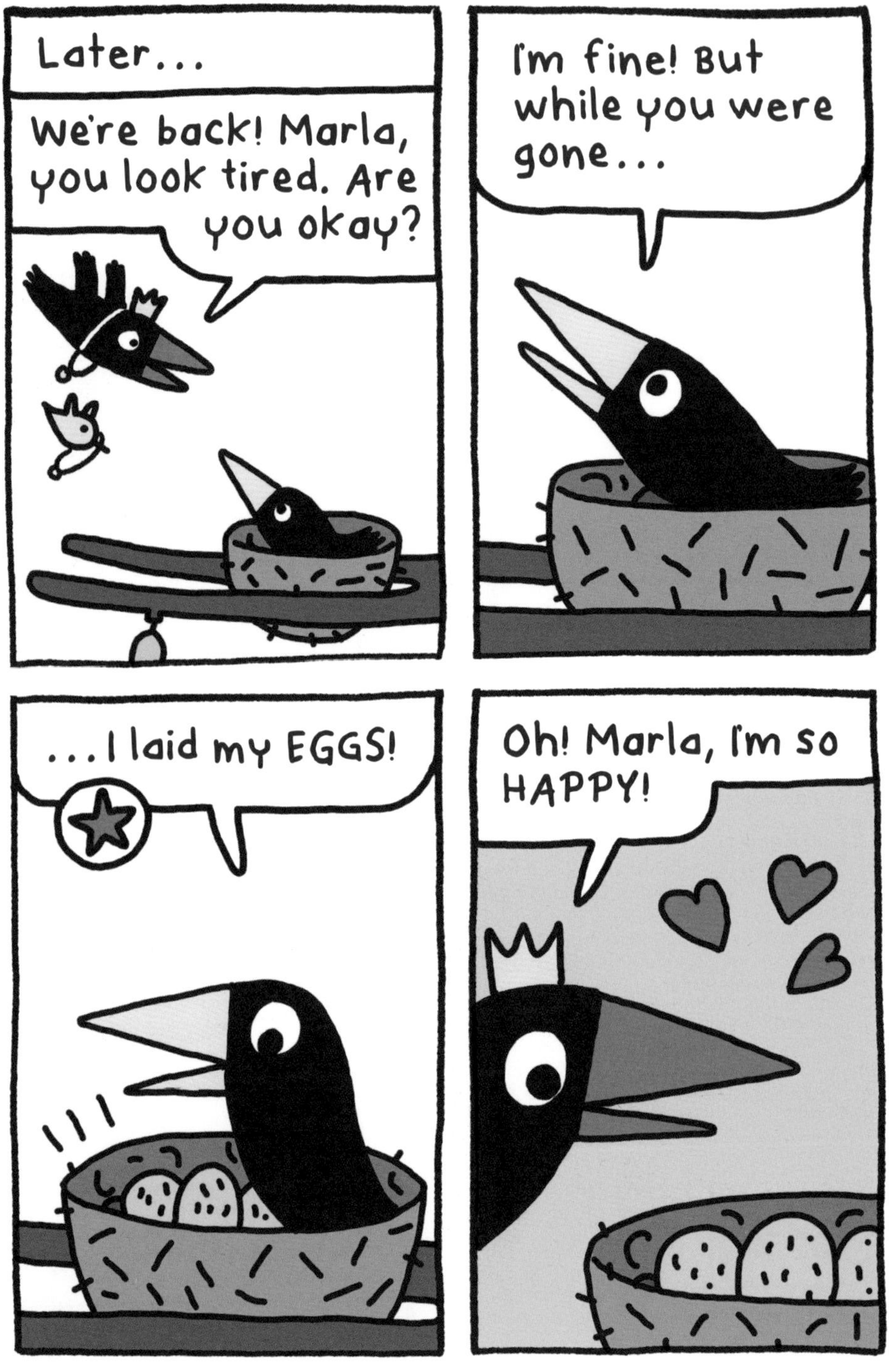
Later...
We're back! Marla, you look tired. Are you okay?
I'm fine! But while you were gone...
...I laid my EGGS!
Oh! Marla, I'm so HAPPY!

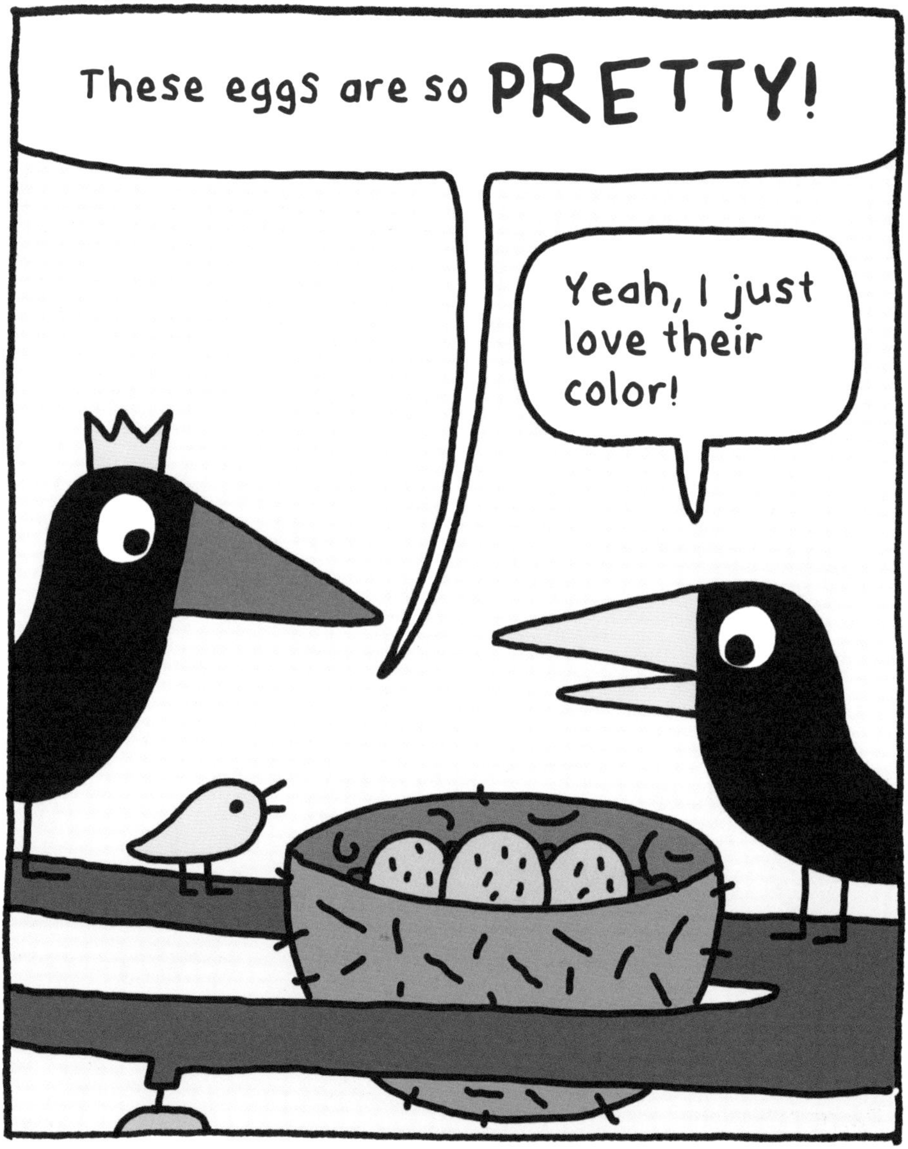
These eggs are so PRETTY!
Yeah, I just love their color!

Crows don't lay eggs that fast. They can lay one a day but sometimes take longer, and I need to keep this story going!

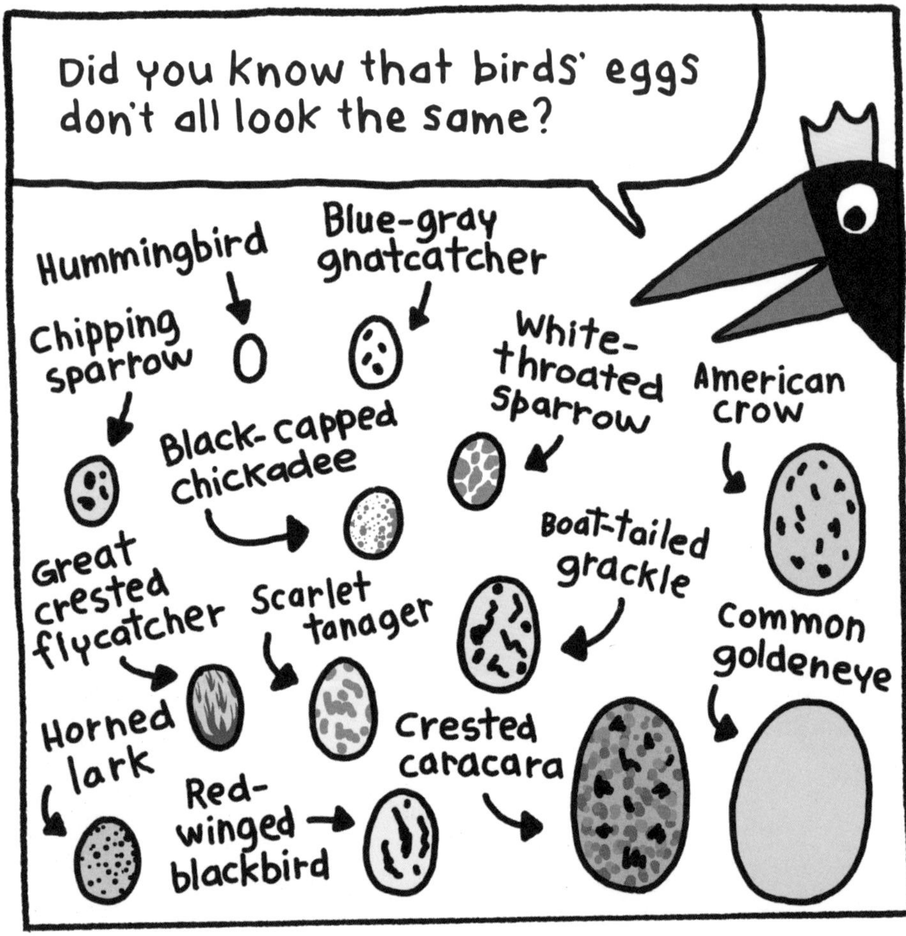
Did you know that birds' eggs don't all look the same?
Hummingbird
Blue-gray gnatcatcher
Chipping sparrow
White-throated sparrow
American crow
Black-capped chickadee
Boat-tailed grackle
Great crested flycatcher
Scarlet tanager
Common goldeneye
Horned lark
Crested caracara
Red-winged blackbird

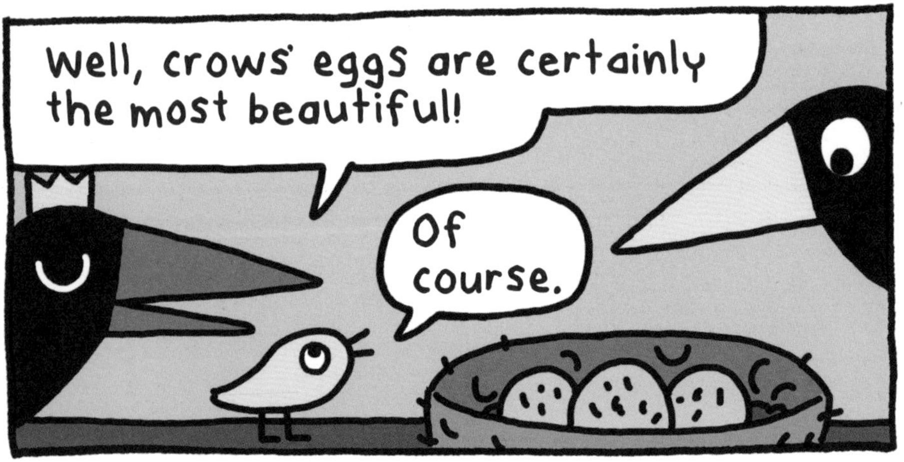
Well, crows' eggs are certainly the most beautiful!
Of course.

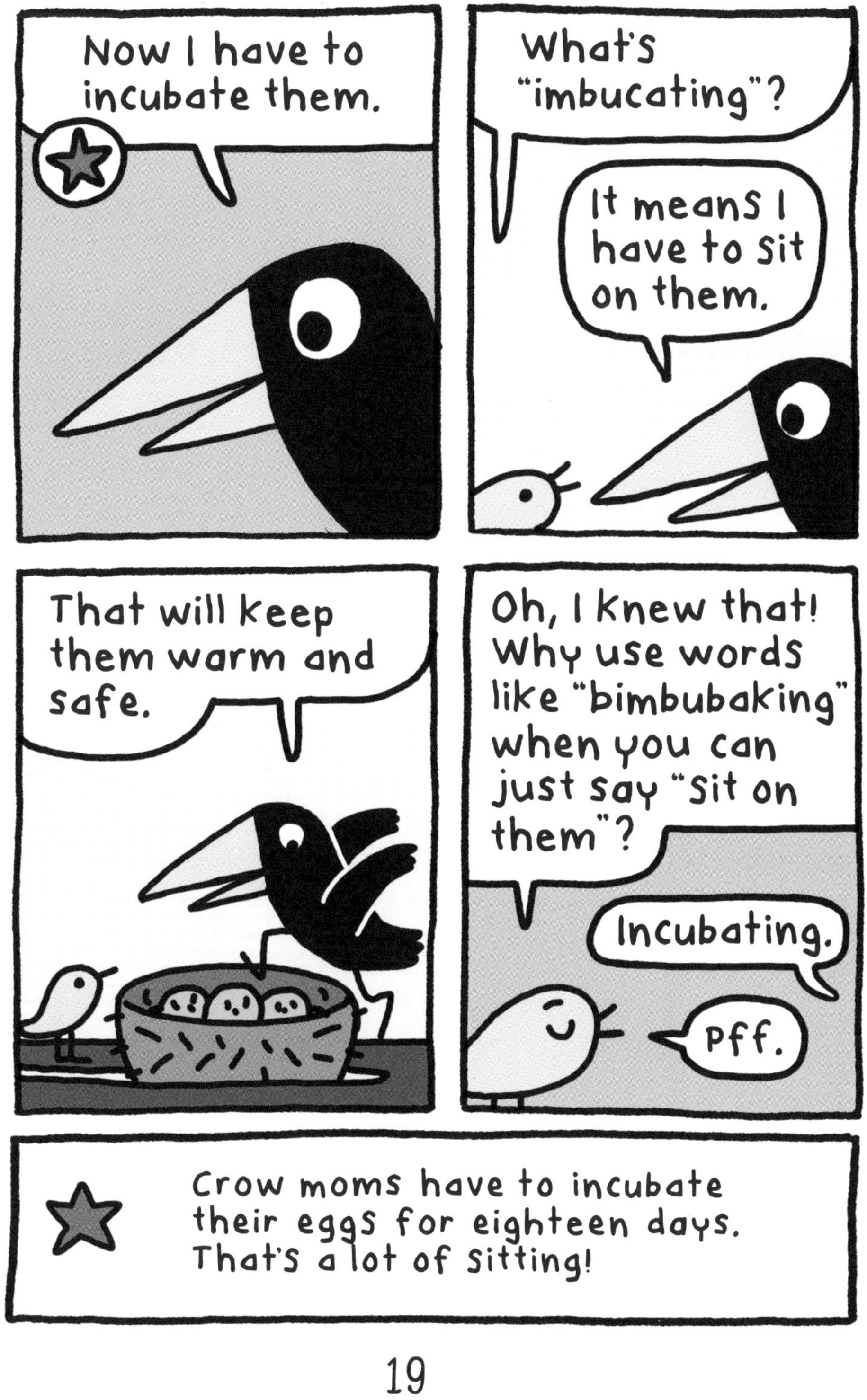
Now I have to incubate them.
What's "imbucating"?
It means I have to sit on them.
That will keep them warm and safe.
Oh, I knew that! Why use words like "bimbubaking" when you can just say "sit on them"?
Incubating.
Pff.

★ Crow moms have to incubate their eggs for eighteen days. That's a lot of sitting!

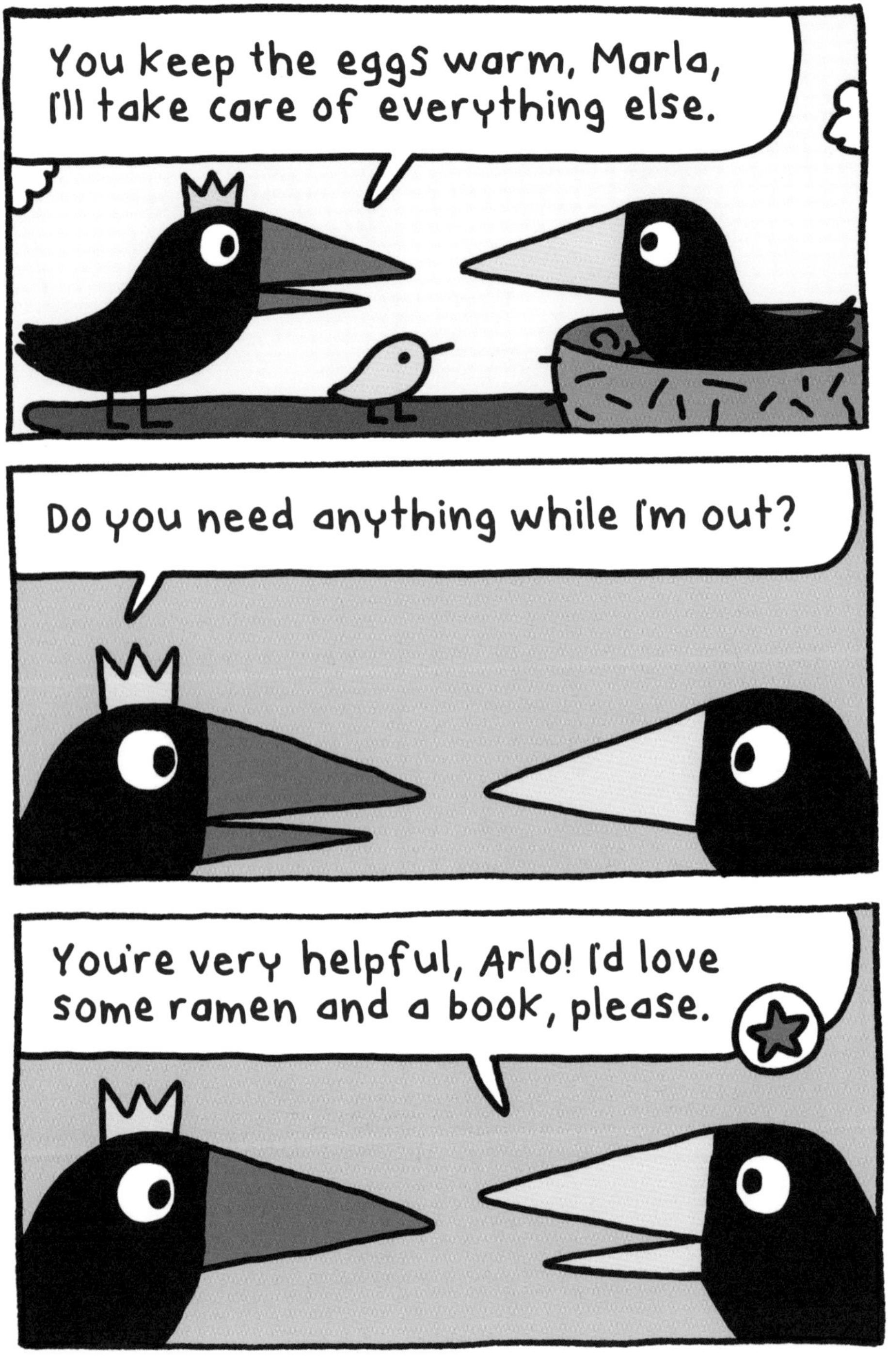
You keep the eggs warm, Marla, I'll take care of everything else.
Do you need anything while I'm out?
You're very helpful, Arlo! I'd love some ramen and a book, please.

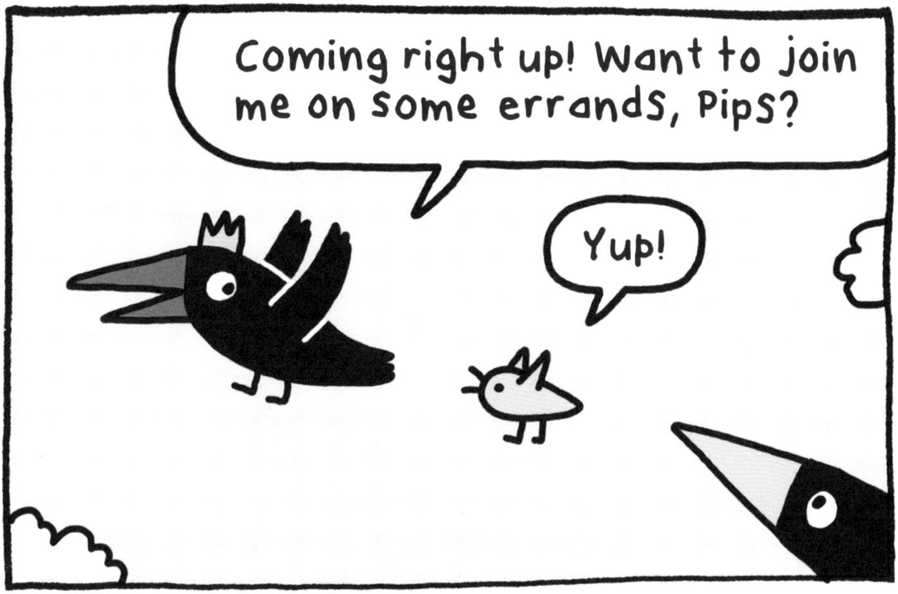
Coming right up! Want to join me on some errands, Pips?
Yup!

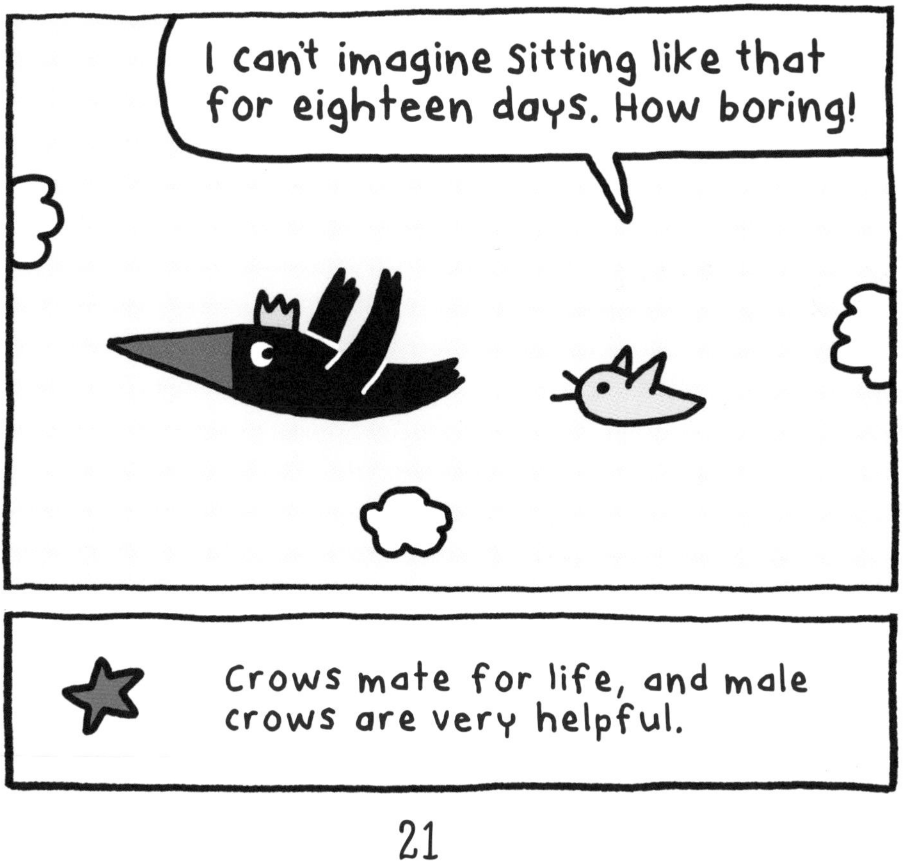
I can't imagine sitting like that for eighteen days. How boring!

Crows mate for life, and male crows are very helpful.

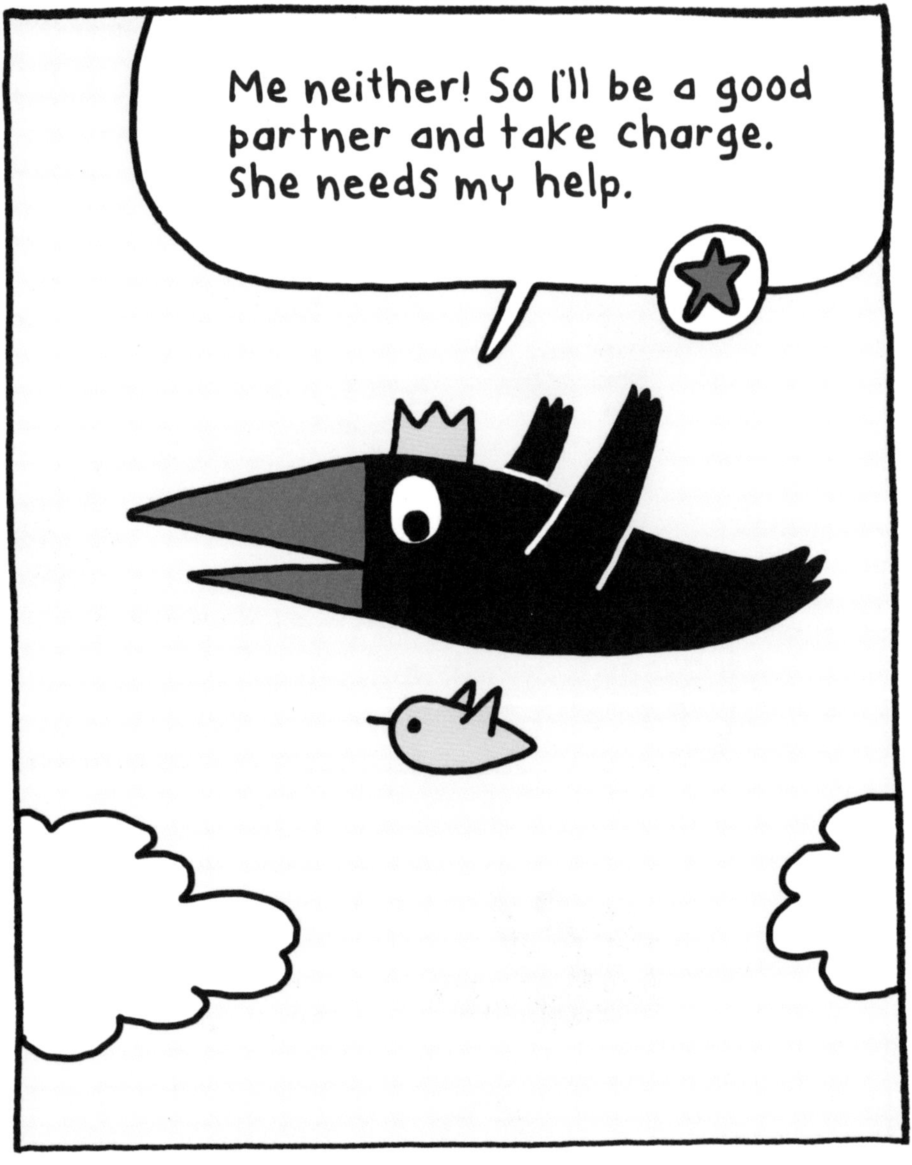
Me neither! So I'll be a good partner and take charge. She needs my help.

Crow dads contribute to the nest and find food for the nesting mom.

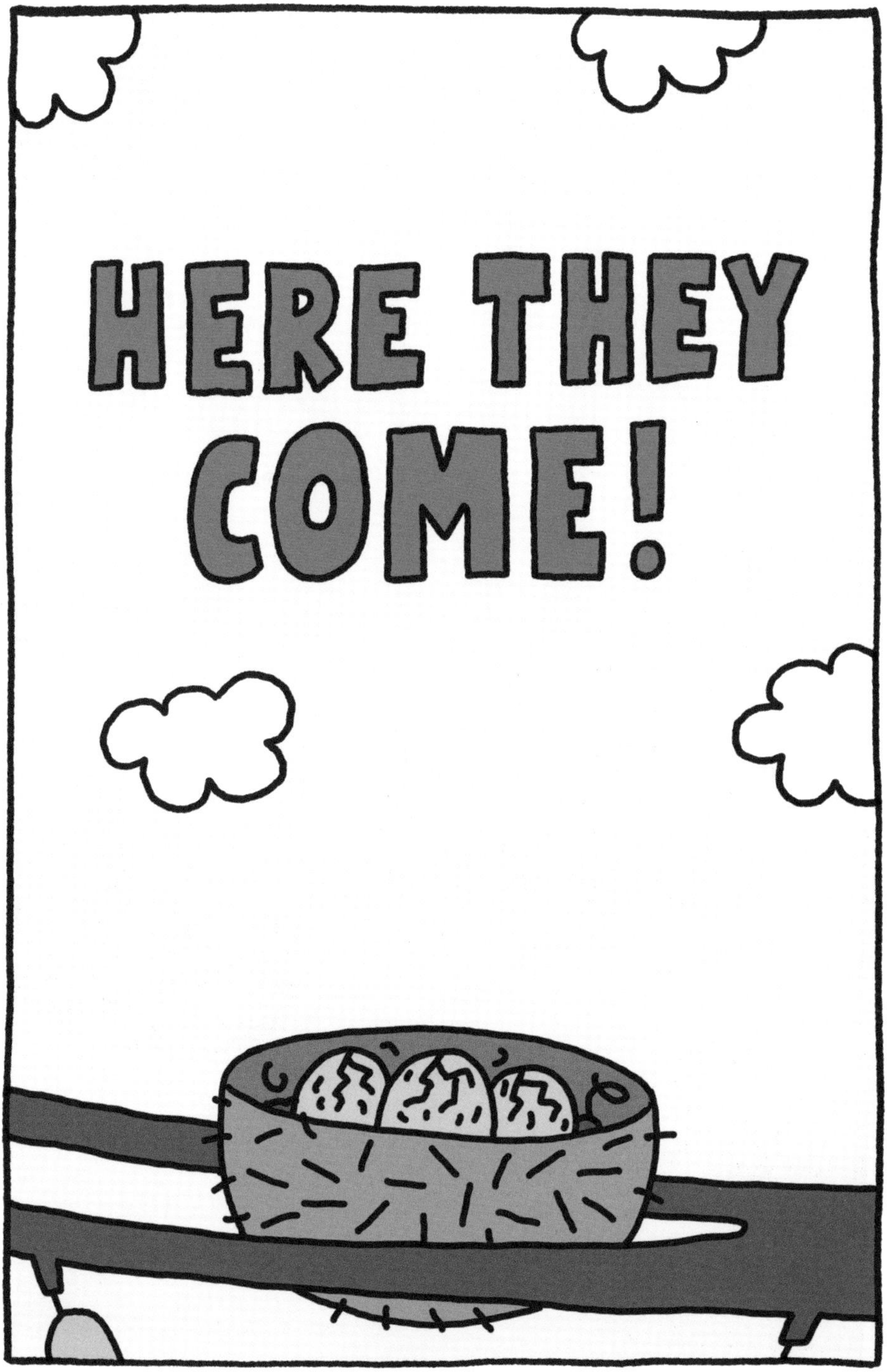
HERE THEY COME!

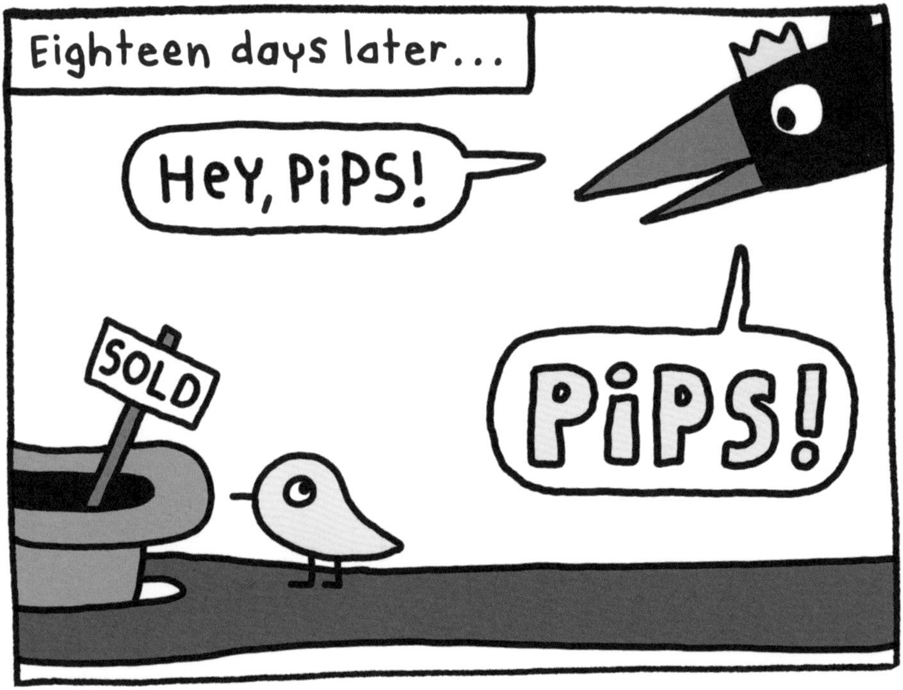
Eighteen days later...
Hey, PiPS!
SOLD
PiPS!

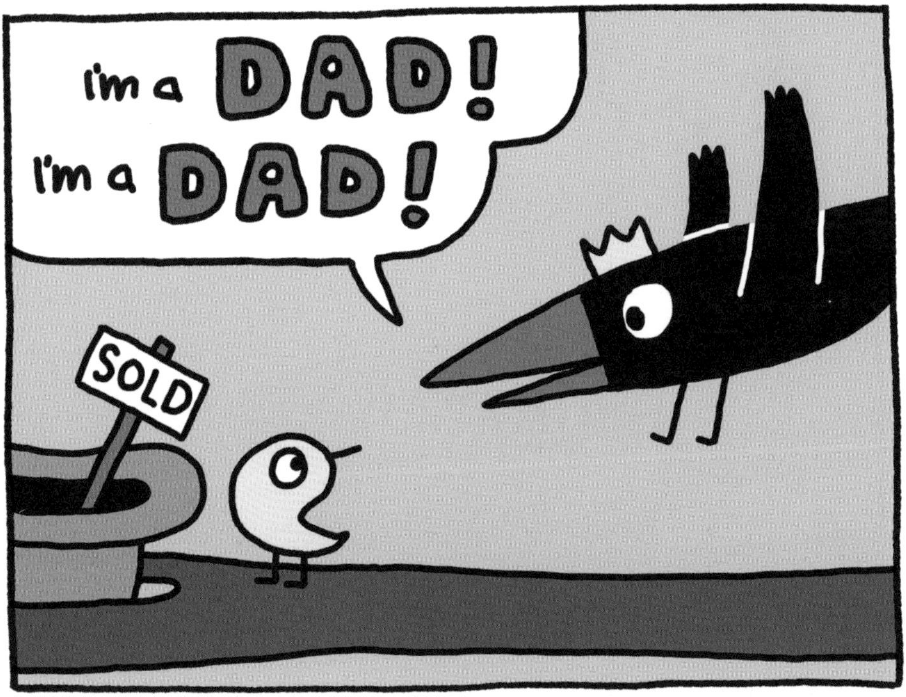
I'm a DAD!
I'm a DAD!
SOLD

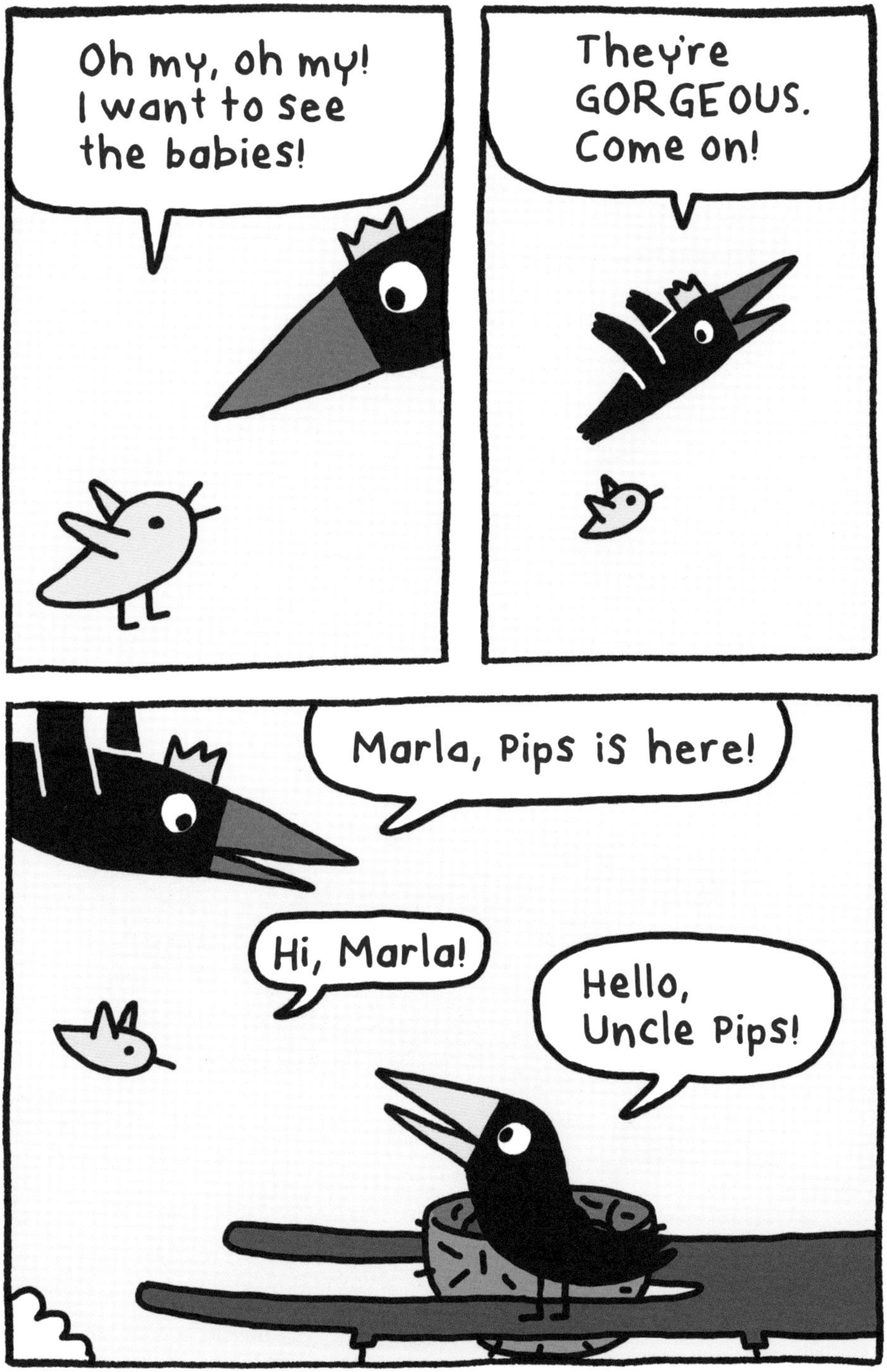
Oh my, oh my! I want to see the babies!
They're GORGEOUS. Come on!
Marla, Pips is here!
Hi, Marla!
Hello, Uncle Pips!

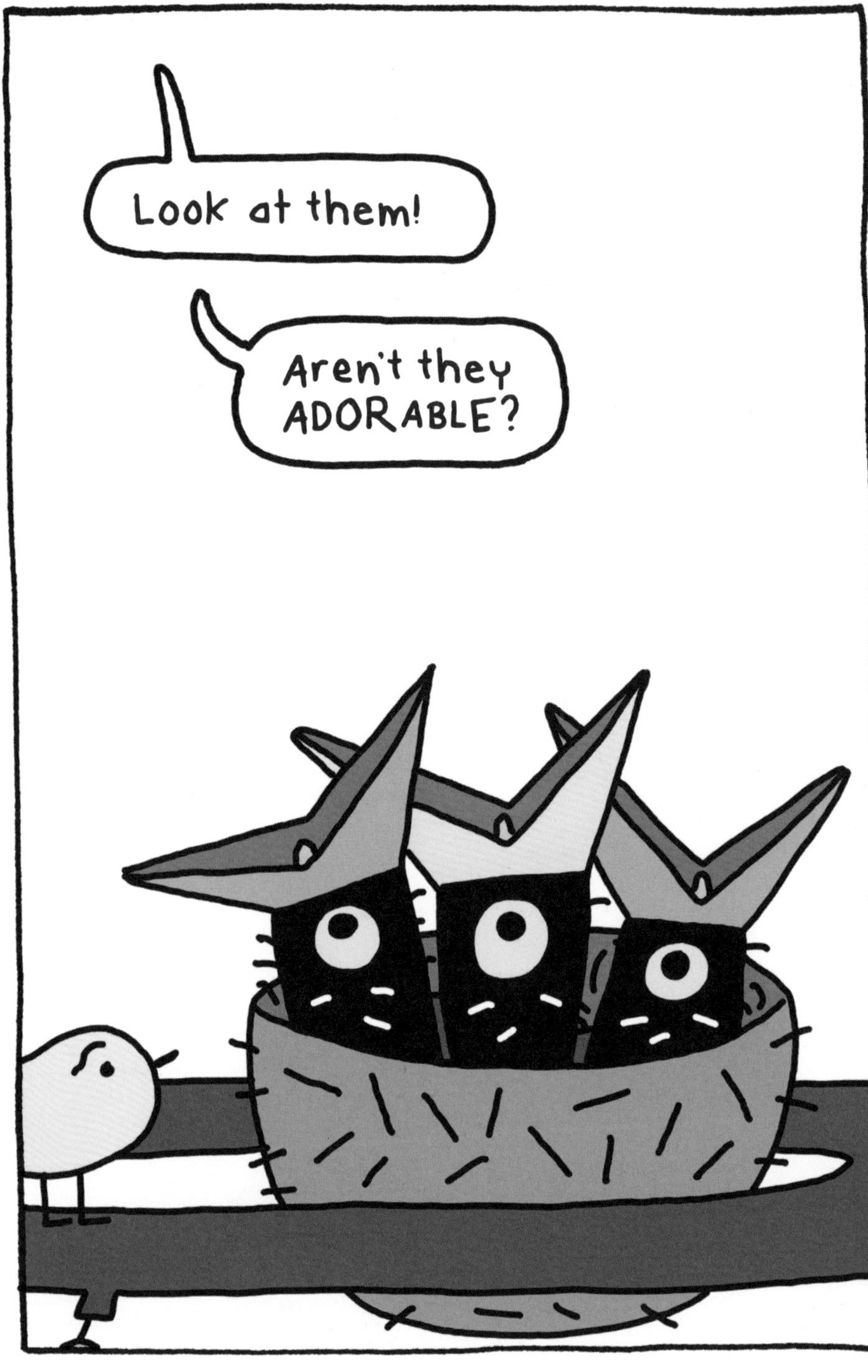
Look at them!
Aren't they ADORABLE?

Yes, they are, um, interesting!
Heh heh.
Nice blue eyes!
Yes, and they look so SMART, don't they?
Yes, clearly geniuses!
Do they have names?

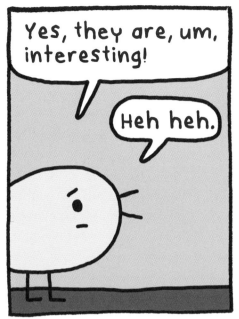

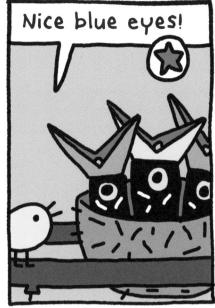

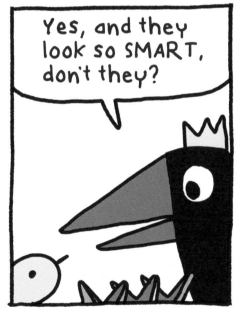

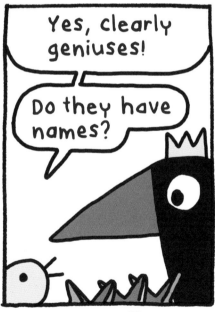

★ Newborn crows have blue eyes that turn black as they grow older.

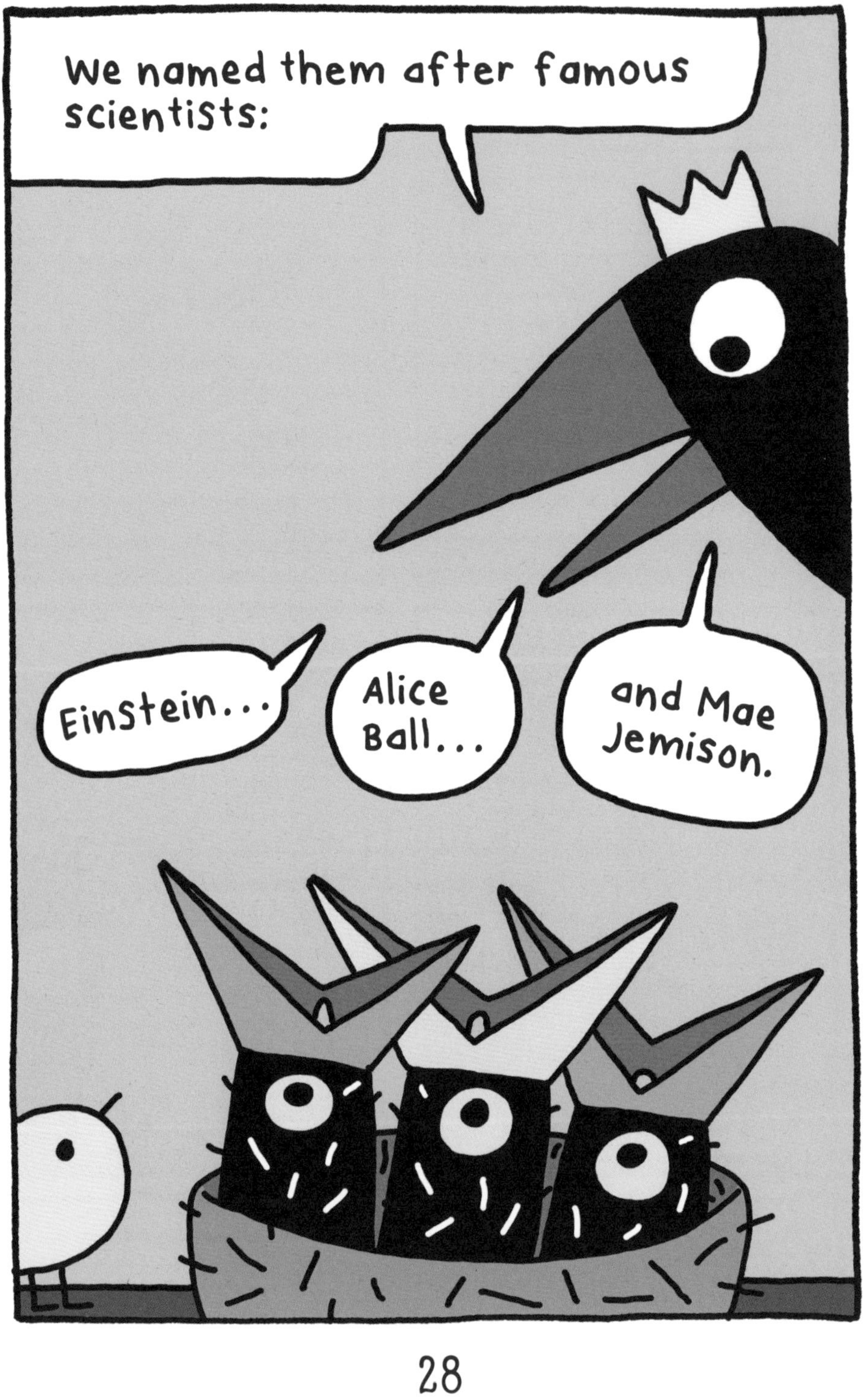
We named them after famous scientists:
Einstein...
Alice Ball...
and Mae Jemison.

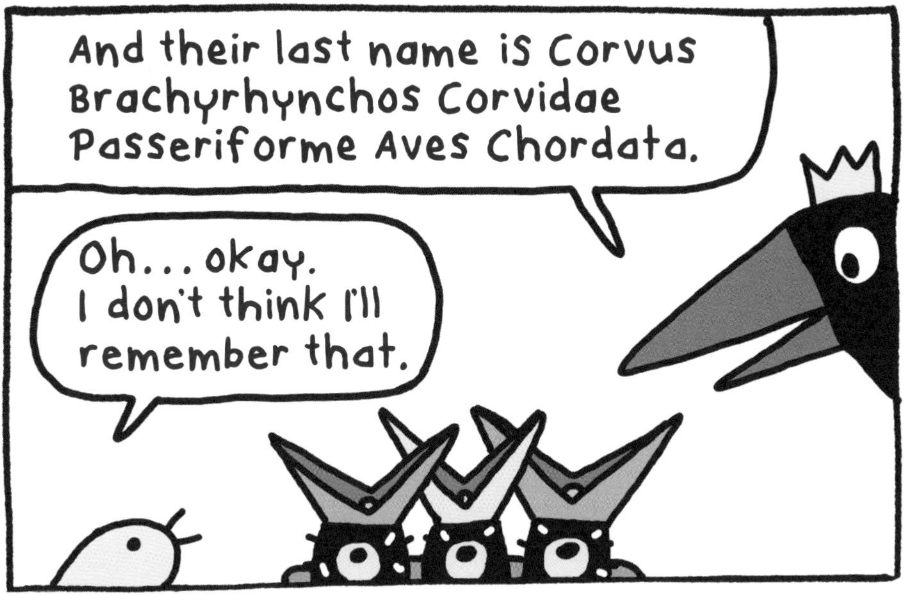
And their last name is Corvus Brachyrhynchos Corvidae Passeriforme Aves Chordata.
Oh... okay. I don't think I'll remember that.

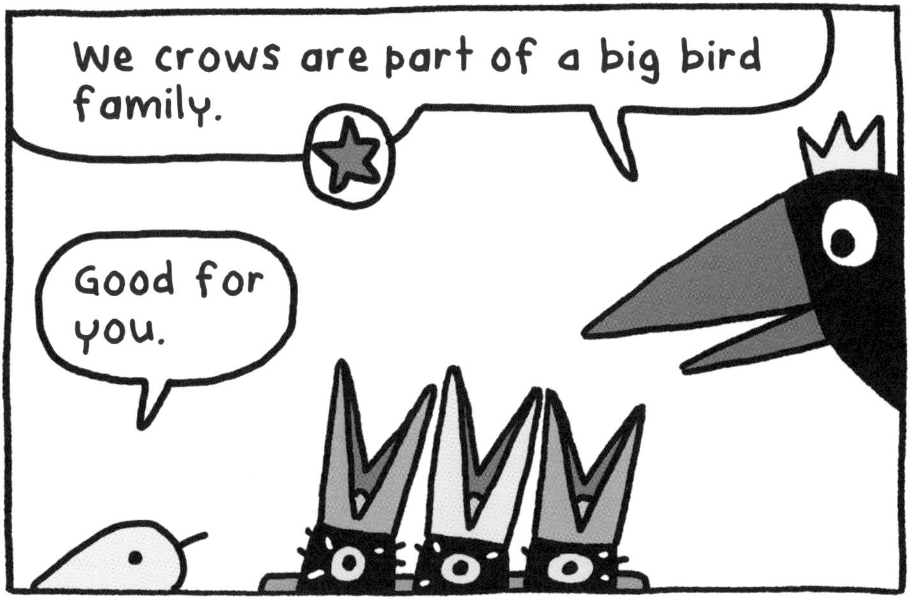
We crows are part of a big bird family.
Good for you.

★ Crows are part of the Corvidae family, which includes ravens, blue jays, magpies, rooks, and nutcrackers.

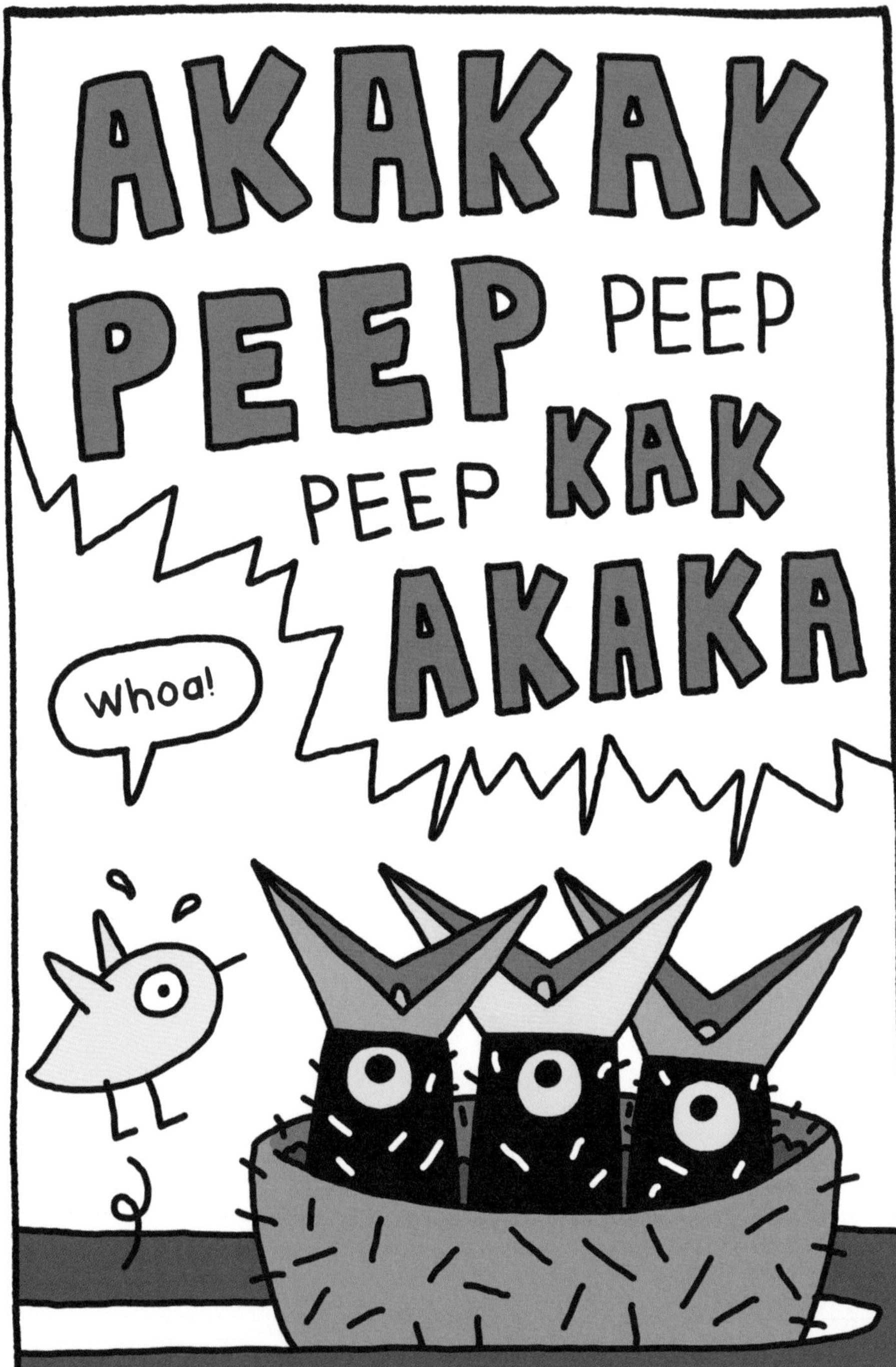
AKAKAK
PEEP PEEP
PEEP KAK
AKAKA
Whoa!

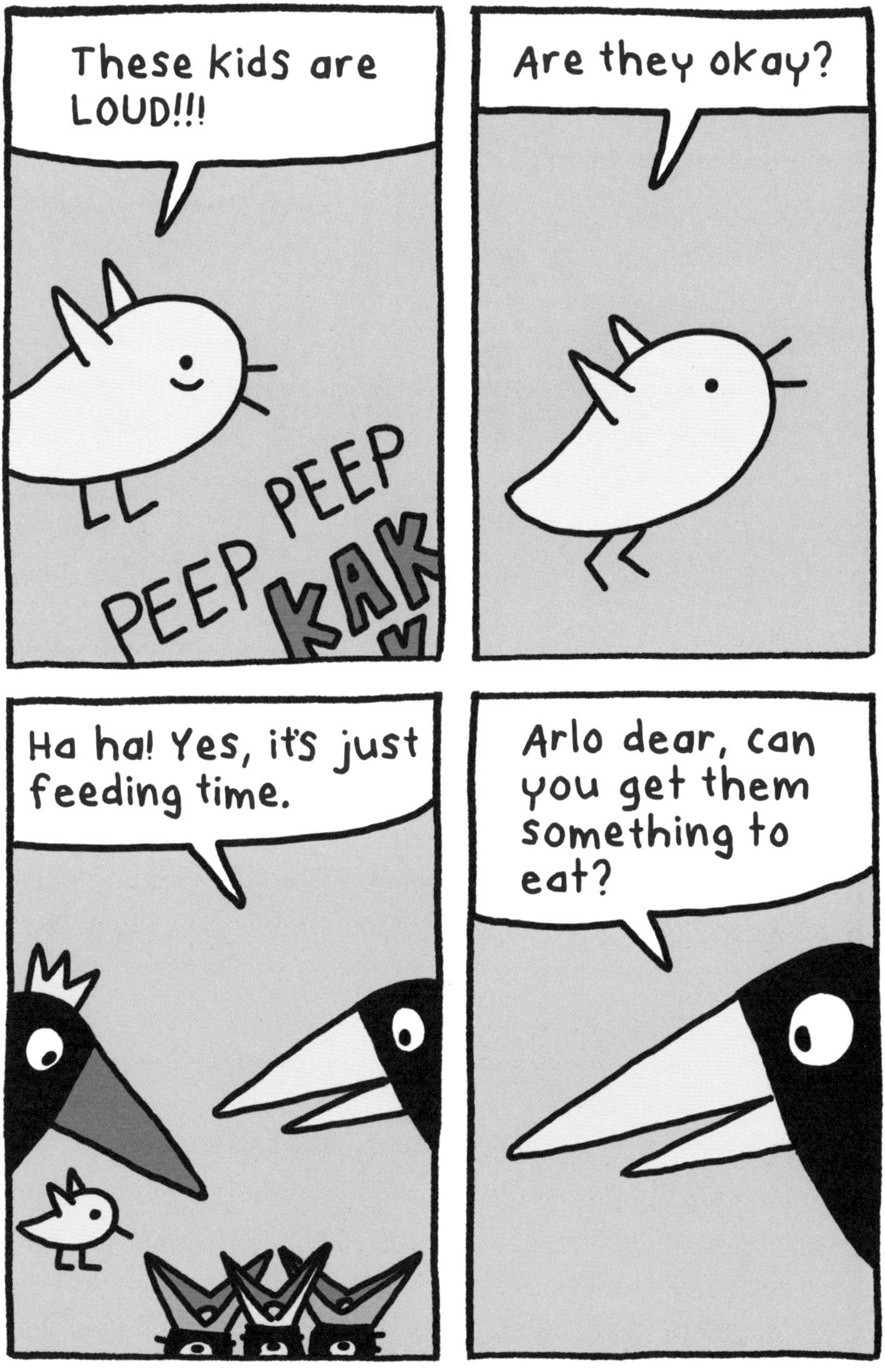
These kids are LOUD!!!
PEEP PEEP
PEEP
KAK
Are they okay?
Ha ha! Yes, it's just feeding time.
Arlo dear, can you get them something to eat?

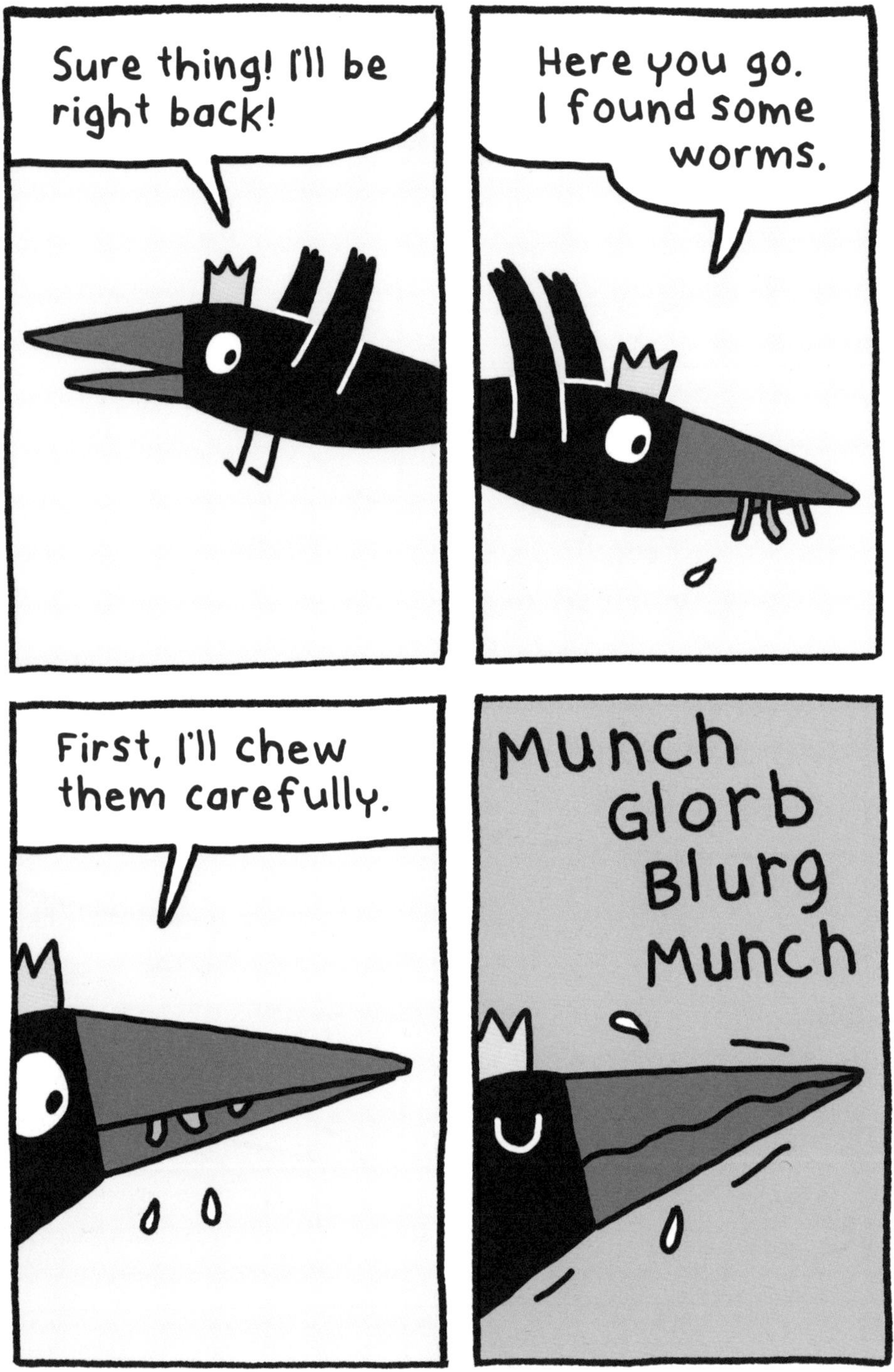
Sure thing! I'll be right back!
Here you go. I found some worms.
First, I'll chew them carefully.
Munch Glorb Blurg Munch

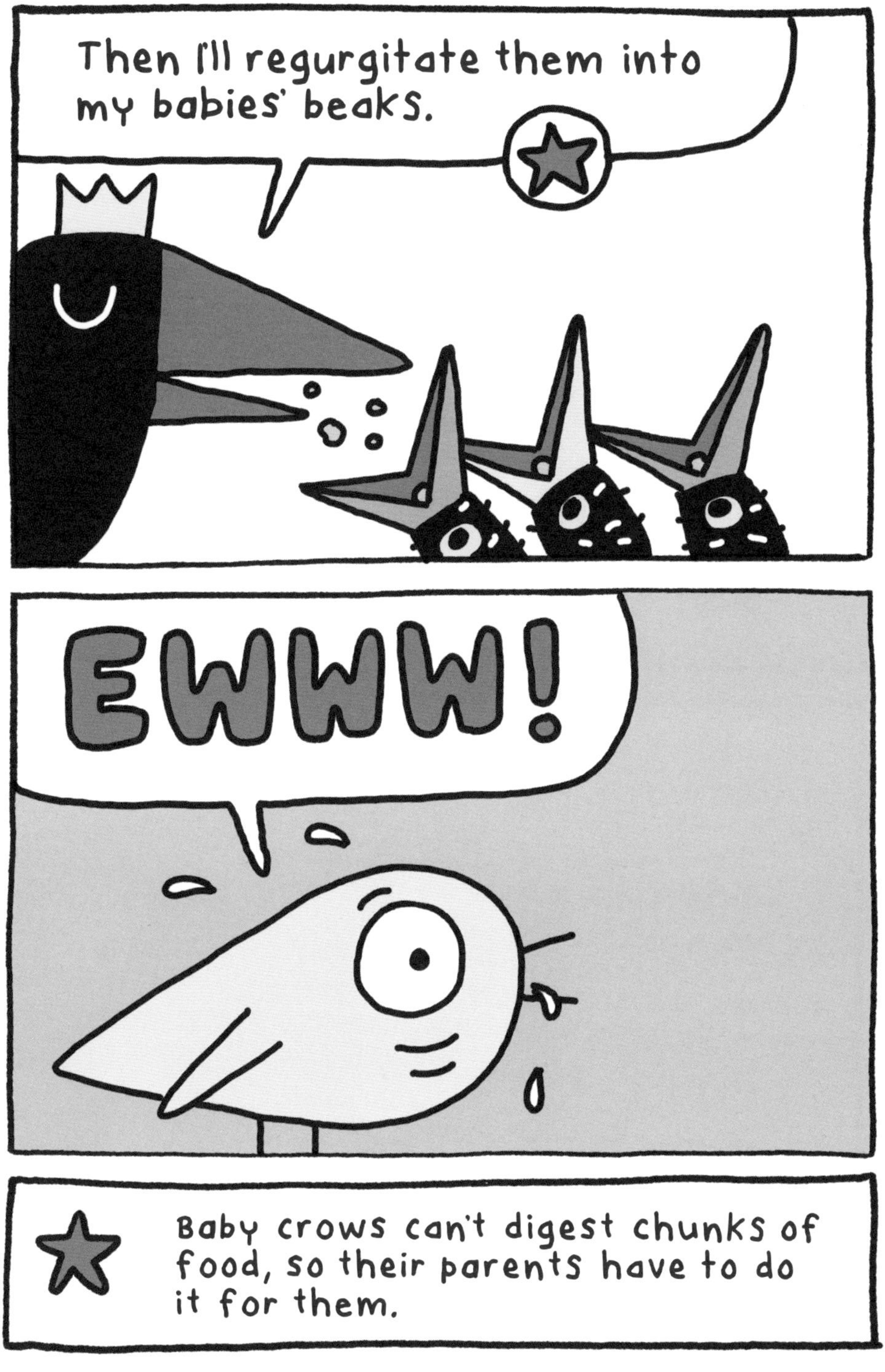
Then I'll regurgitate them into my babies' beaks.
EWWW!
Baby crows can't digest chunks of food, so their parents have to do it for them.

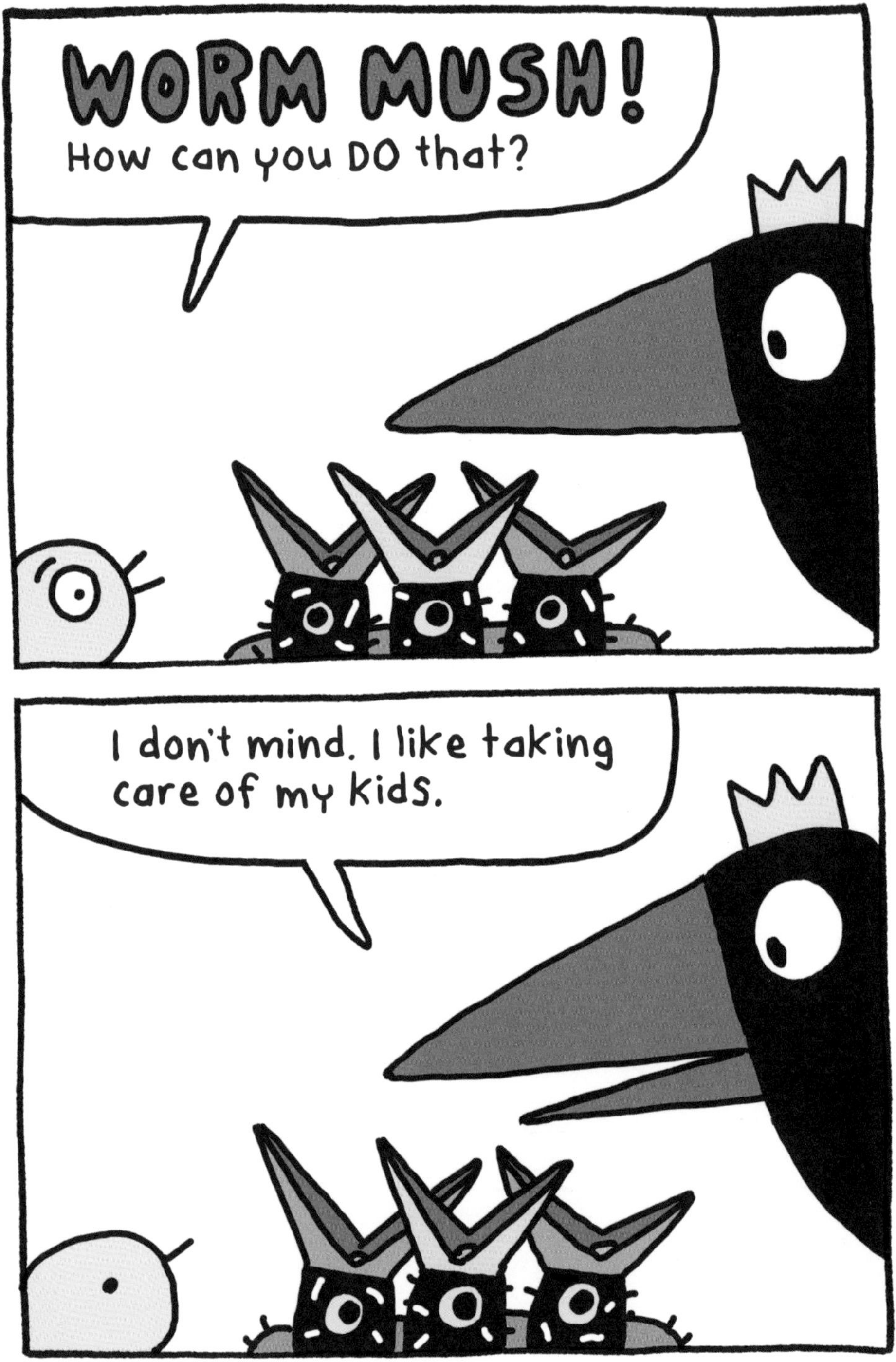
WORM MUSH!
How can you DO that?
I don't mind. I like taking care of my kids.

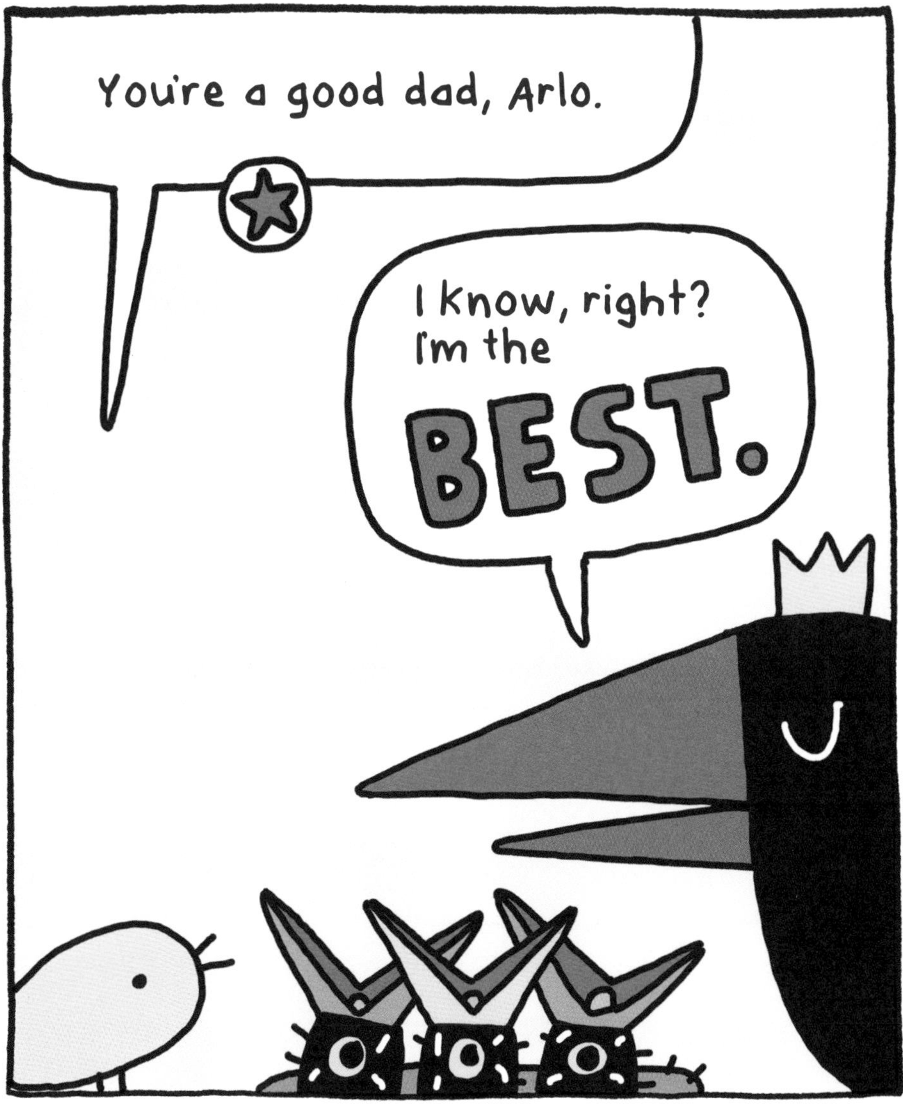
You're a good dad, Arlo.
I know, right? I'm the BEST.

★ Unlike other bird species, crow dads are good parents. They help feed and educate their babies.

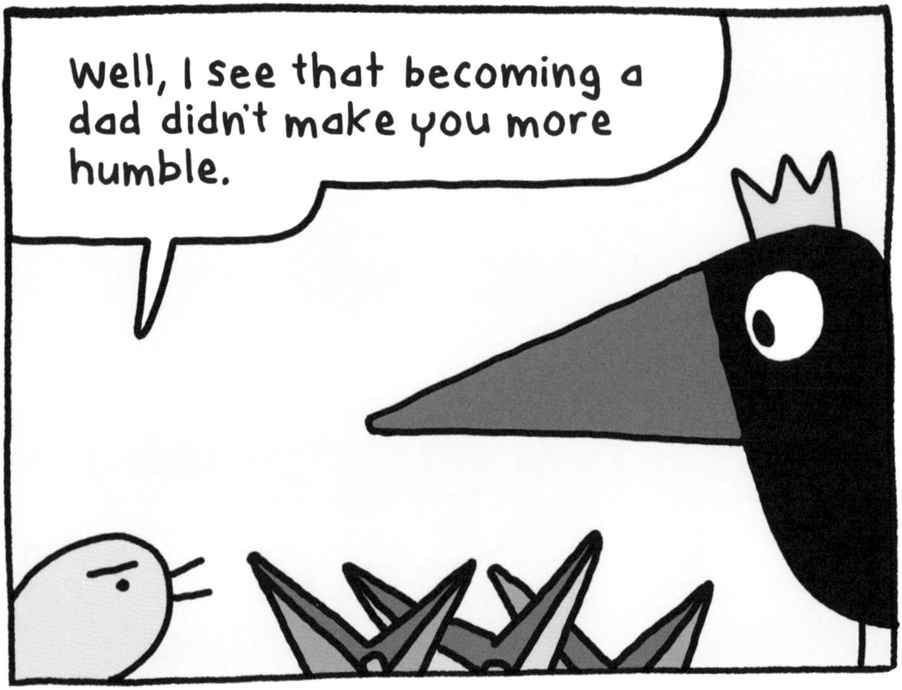
Well, I see that becoming a dad didn't make you more humble.

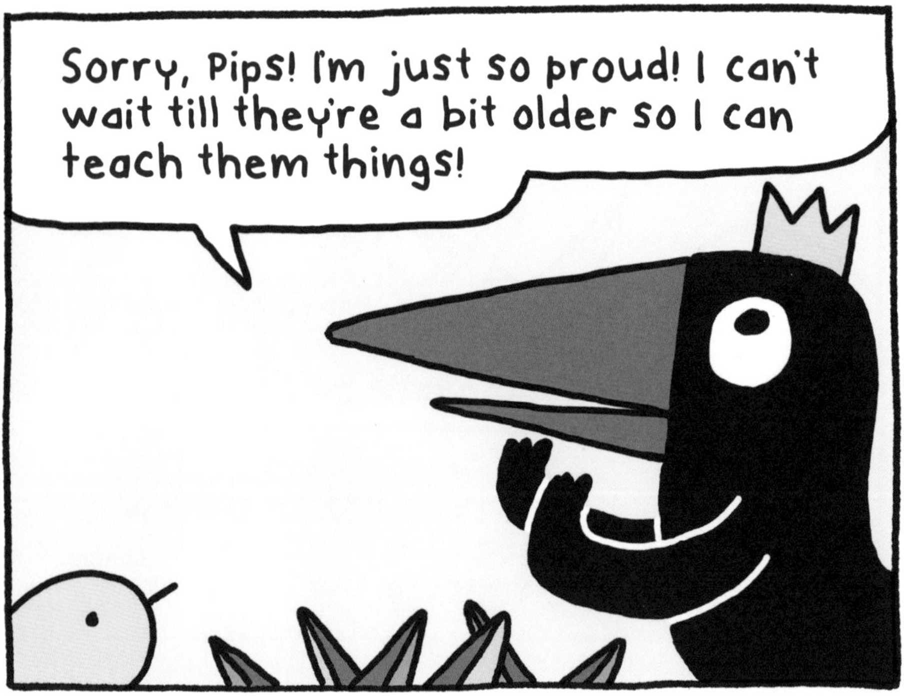
Sorry, Pips! I'm just so proud! I can't wait till they're a bit older so I can teach them things!

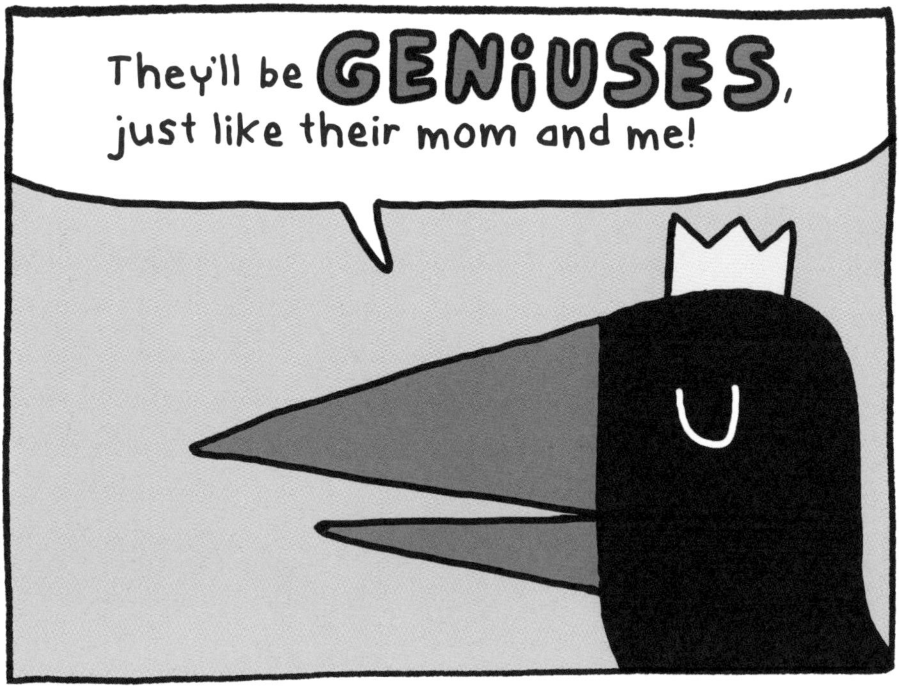
They'll be GENIUSES, just like their mom and me!

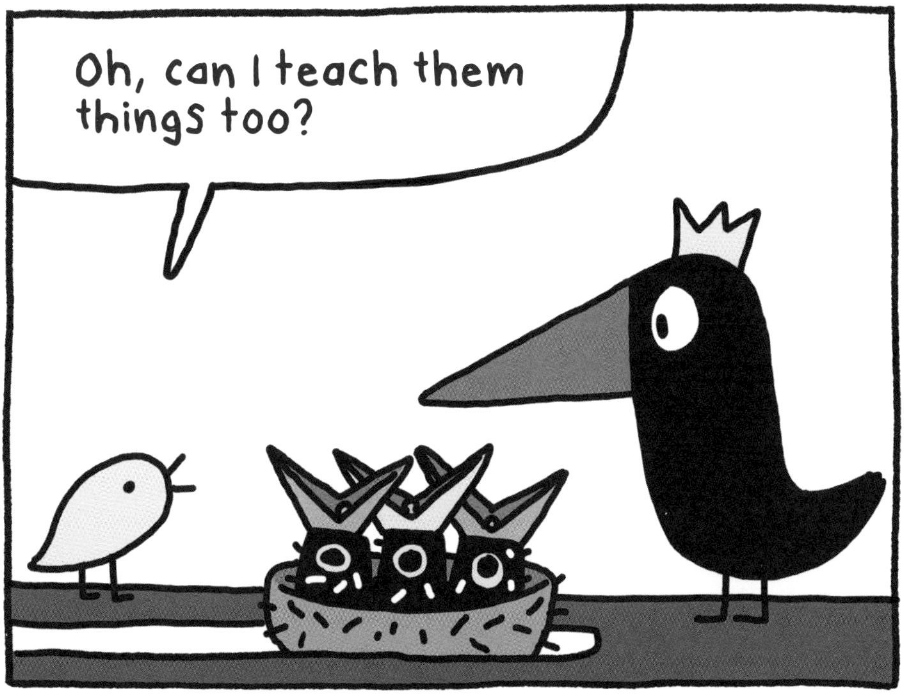
Oh, can I teach them things too?

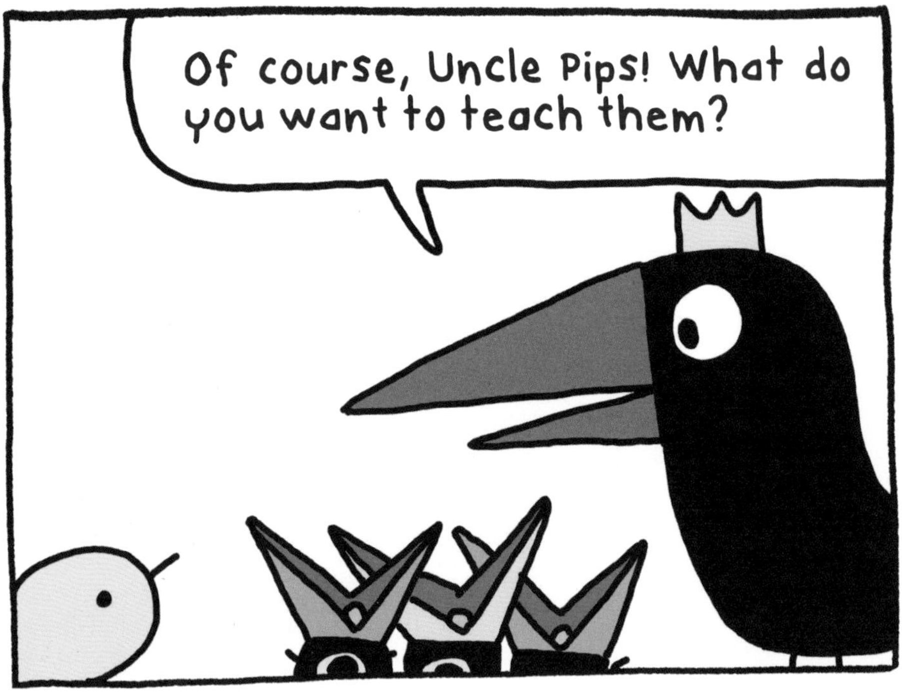
Of course, Uncle Pips! What do you want to teach them?

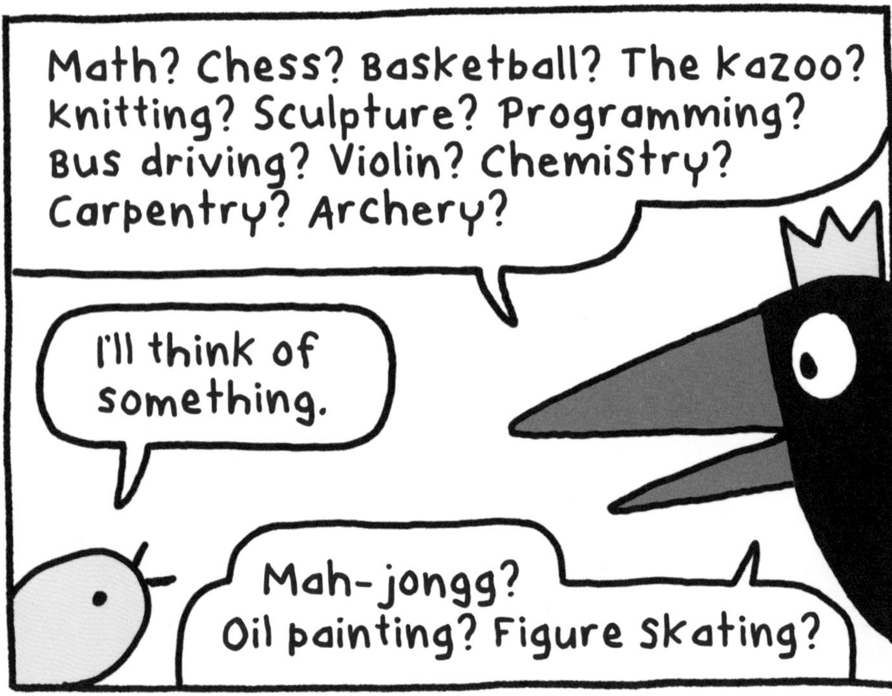
Math? Chess? Basketball? The kazoo? Knitting? Sculpture? Programming? Bus driving? Violin? Chemistry? Carpentry? Archery?
I'll think of something.
Mah-jongg? Oil painting? Figure skating?

HOME SCHOOL

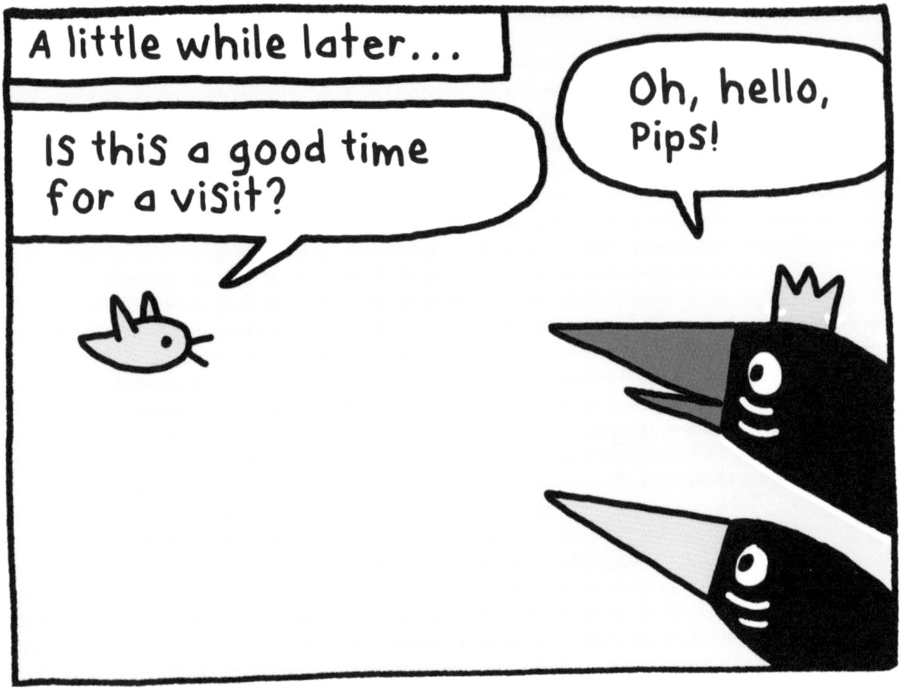
A little while later...
Is this a good time for a visit?
Oh, hello, Pips!

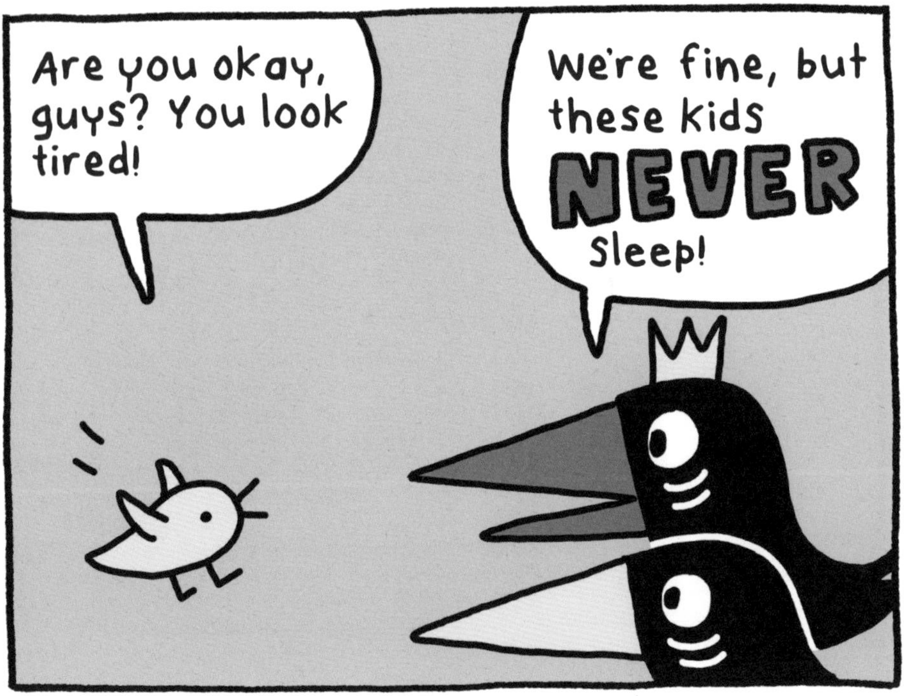
Are you okay, guys? You look tired!
We're fine, but these kids NEVER sleep!

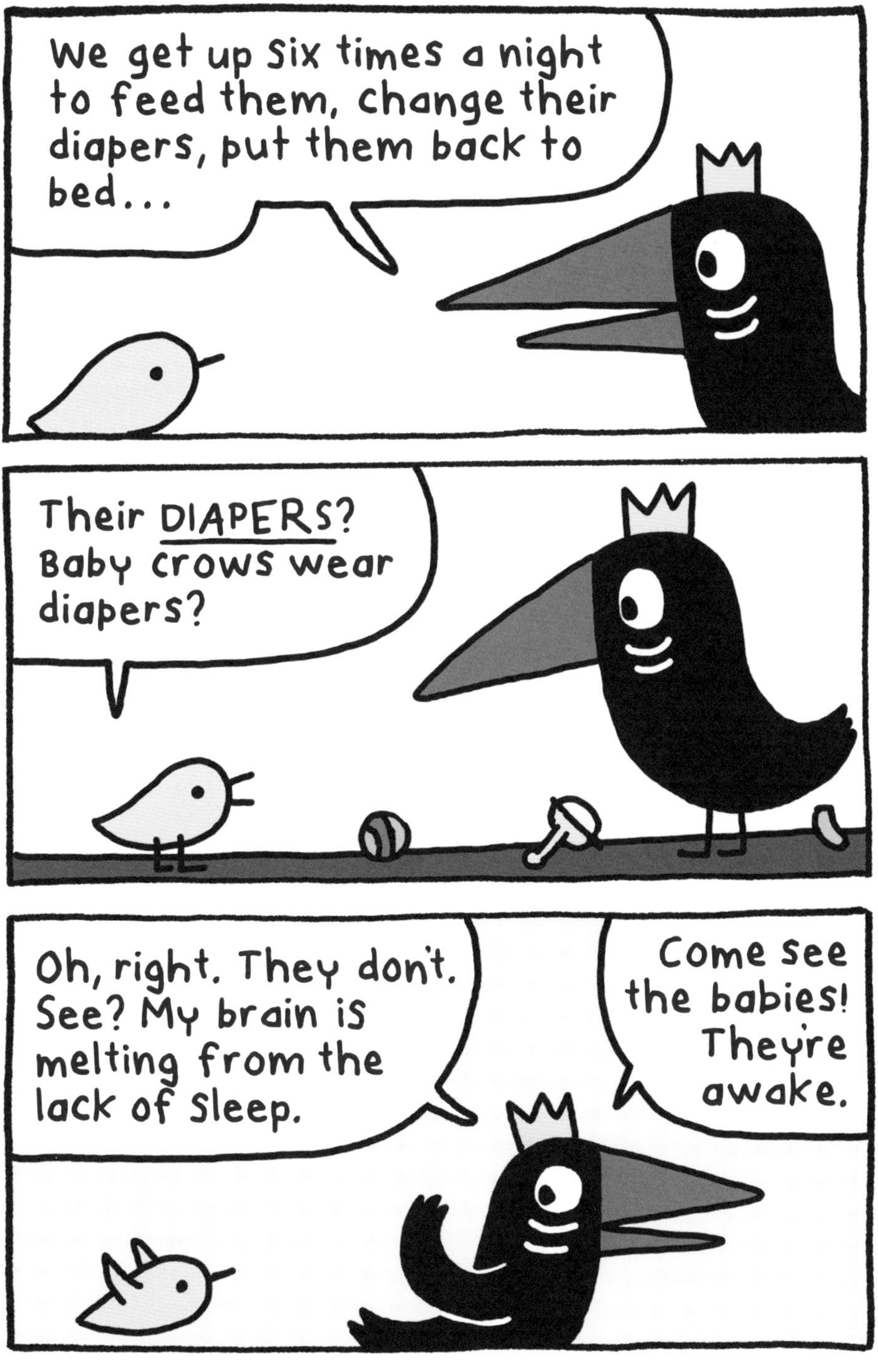
We get up six times a night to feed them, change their diapers, put them back to bed...
Their DIAPERS? Baby crows wear diapers?
Oh, right. They don't. See? My brain is melting from the lack of sleep.
Come see the babies! They're awake.

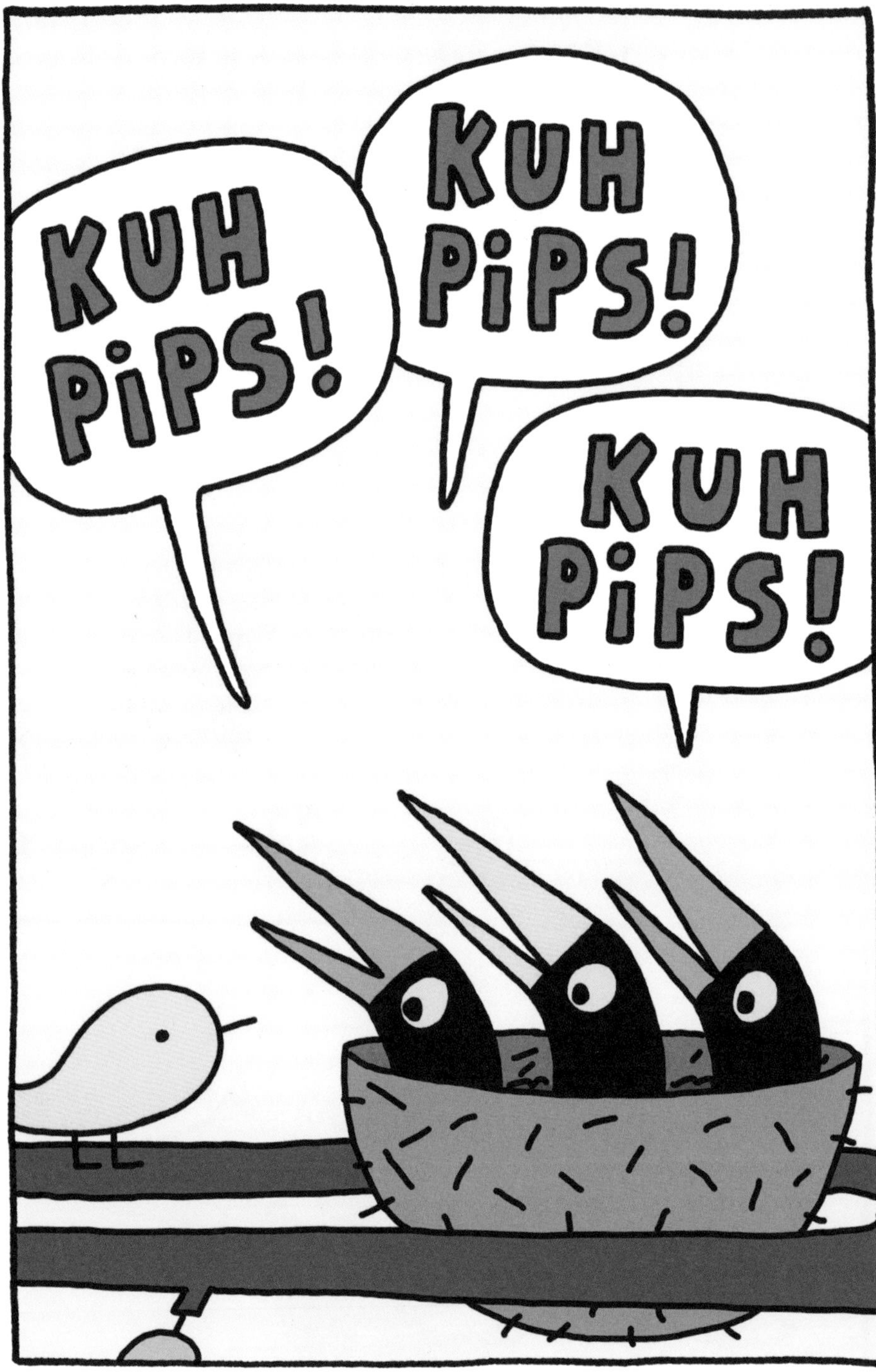
KUH PiPS!
KUH PiPS!
KUH PiPS!

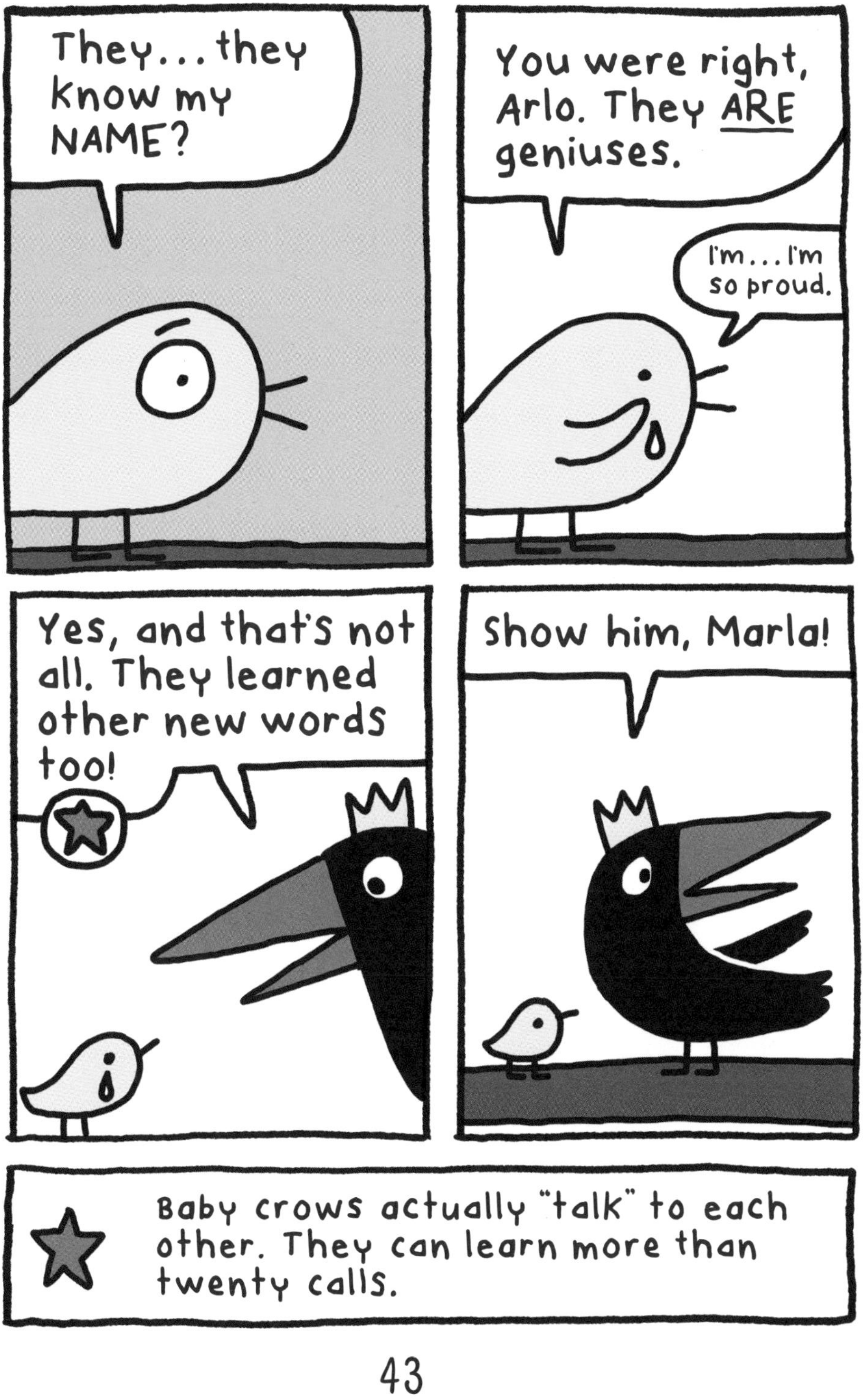
They... they know my NAME?
You were right, Arlo. They ARE geniuses.
I'm... I'm so proud.
Yes, and that's not all. They learned other new words too!
Show him, Marla!

★ Baby crows actually "talk" to each other. They can learn more than twenty calls.

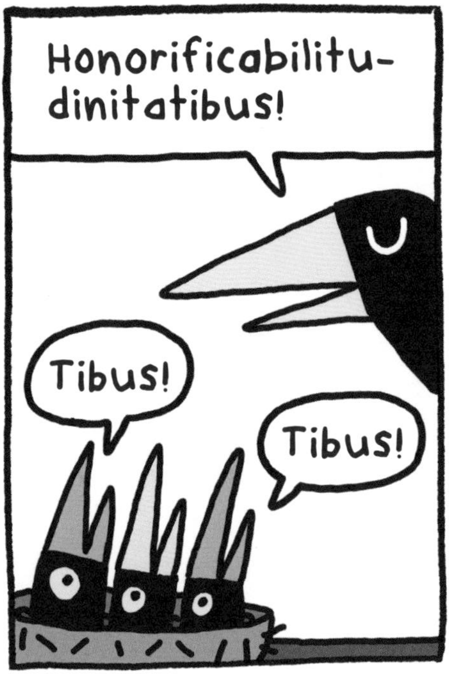
Honorificabilitu-
dinitatibus!
Tibus!
Tibus!

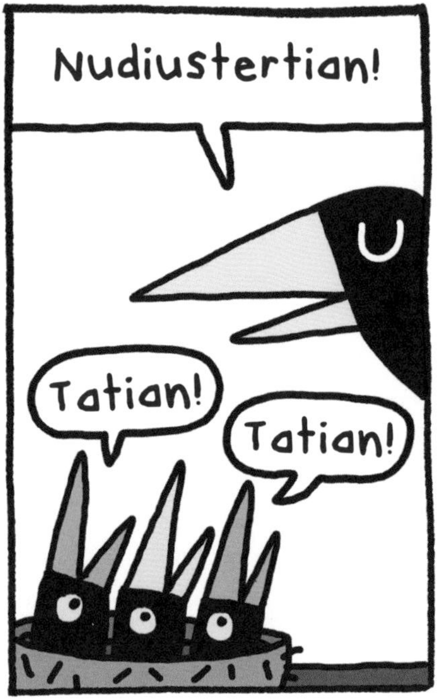
Nudiustertian!
Tatian!
Tatian!

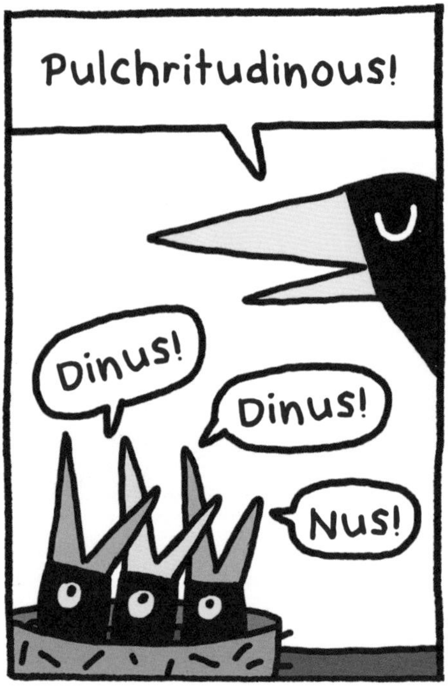
Pulchritudinous!
Dinus!
Dinus!
Nus!

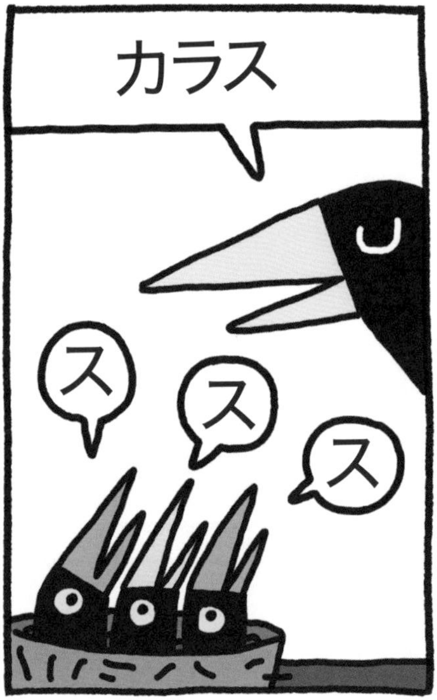
カラス
ス
ス
ス

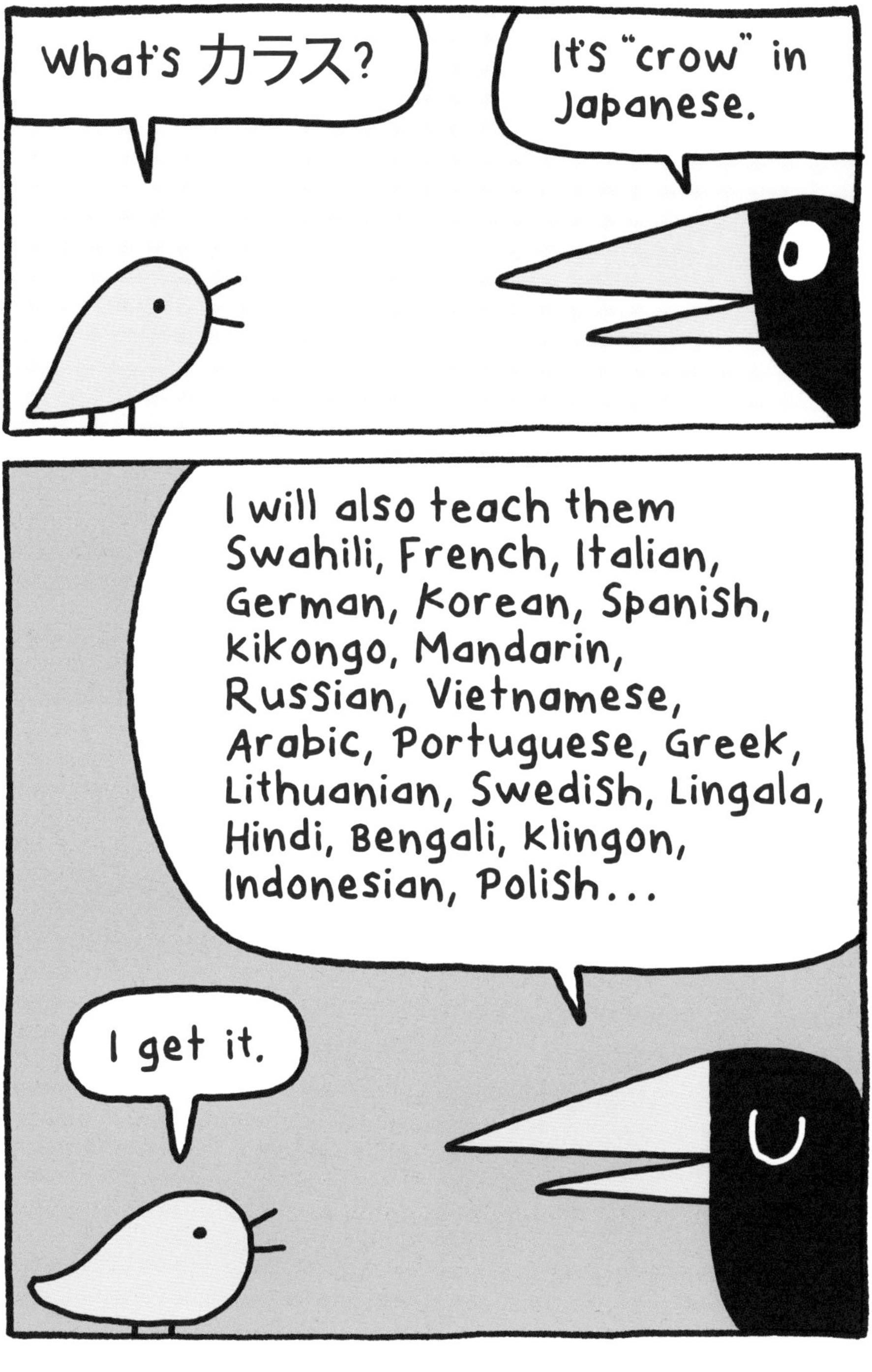
What's カラス?
It's "crow" in Japanese.
I will also teach them Swahili, French, Italian, German, Korean, Spanish, Kikongo, Mandarin, Russian, Vietnamese, Arabic, Portuguese, Greek, Lithuanian, Swedish, Lingala, Hindi, Bengali, Klingon, Indonesian, Polish...
I get it.

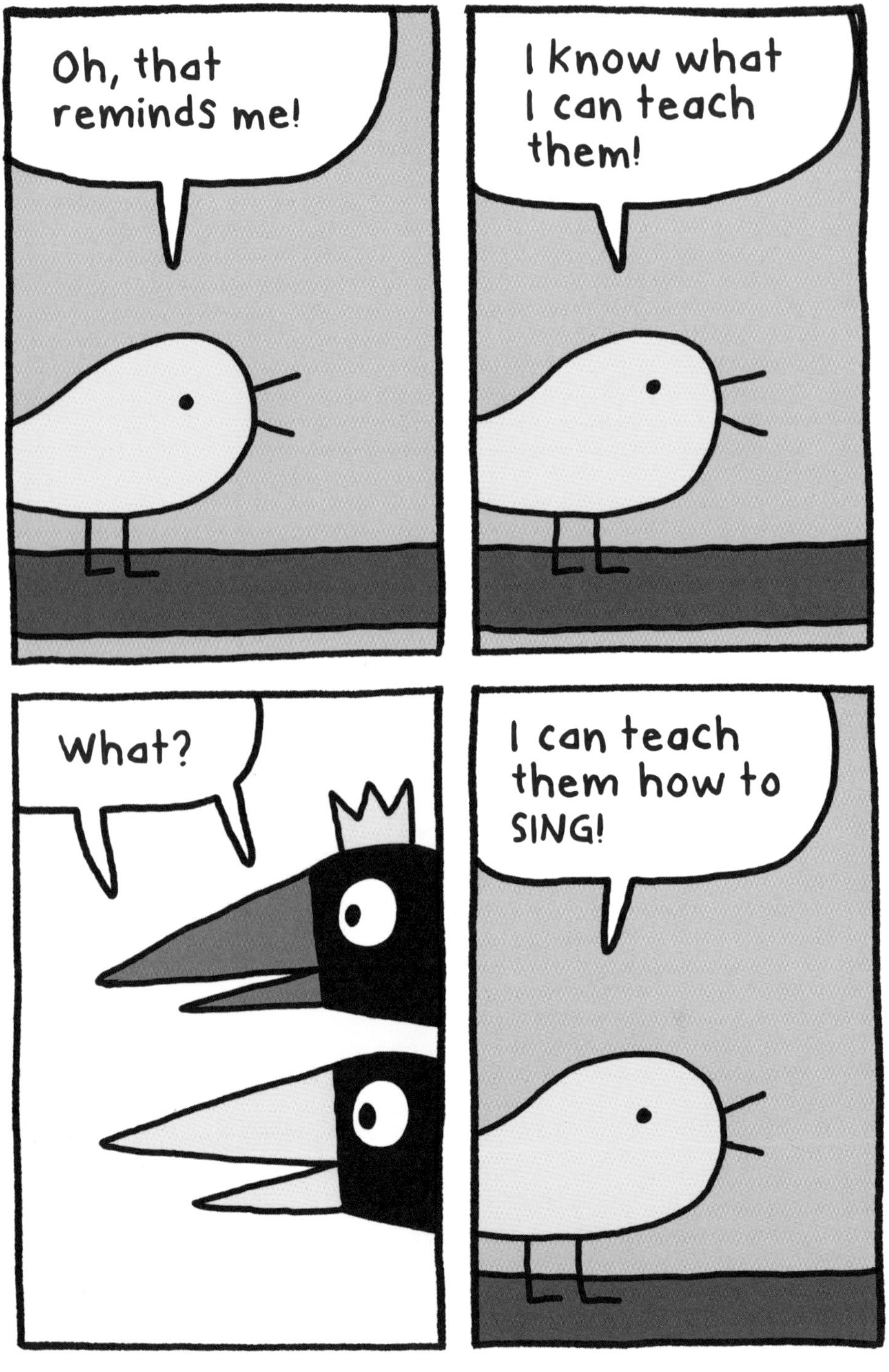
Oh, that reminds me!
I know what I can teach them!
What?
I can teach them how to SING!

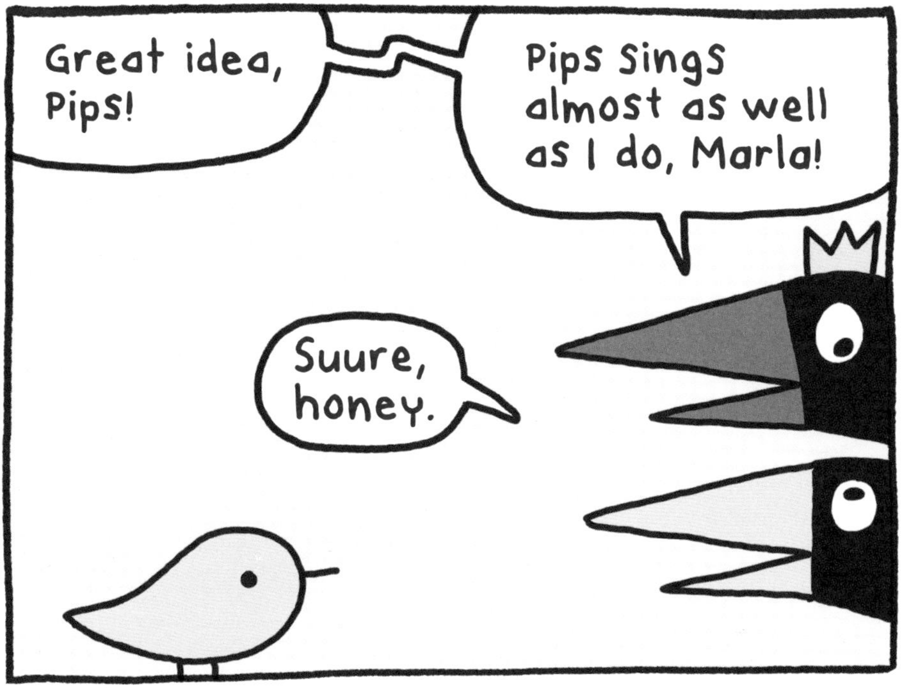
Great idea, Pips!
Pips sings almost as well as I do, Marla!
Suure, honey.

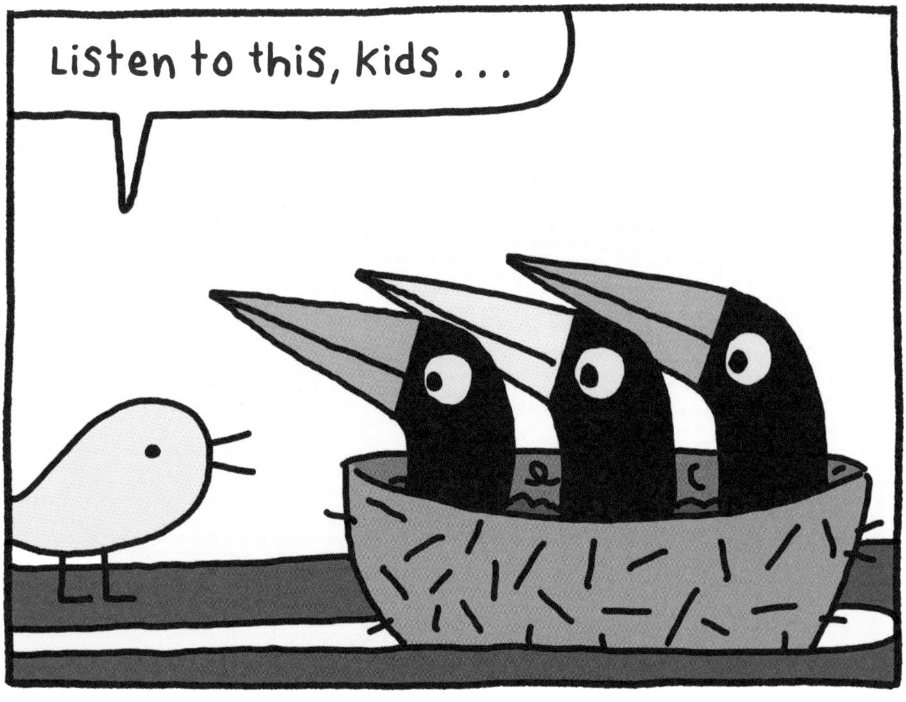
Listen to this, kids . . .

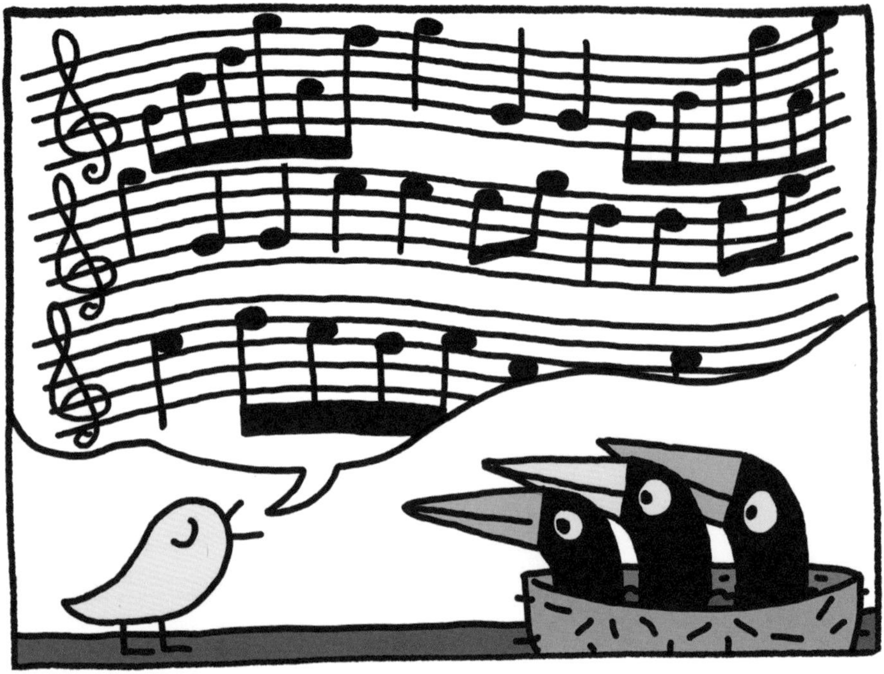

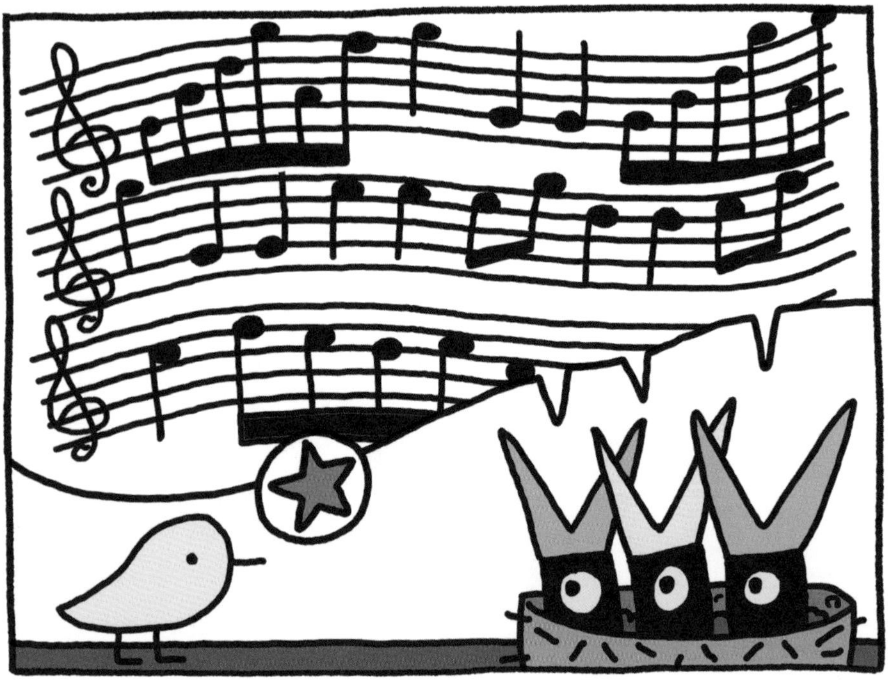

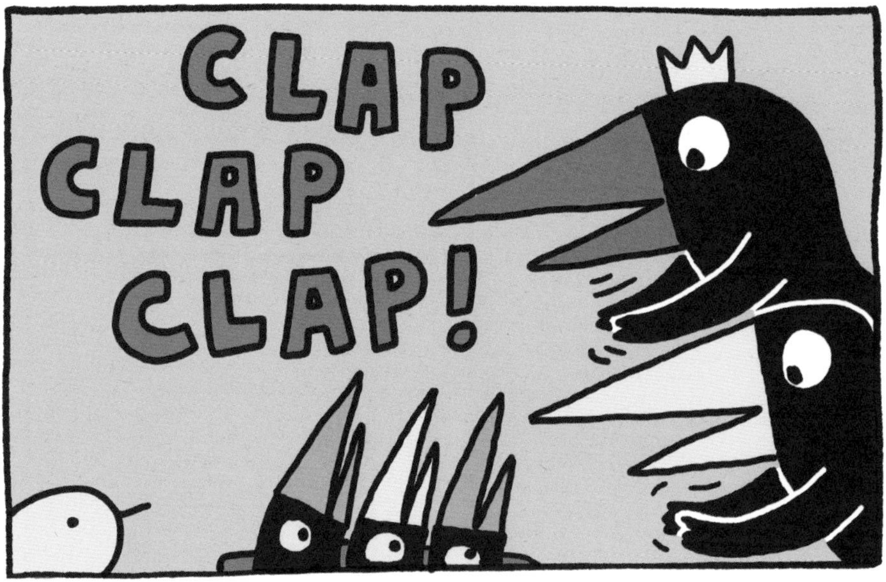
CLAP
CLAP
CLAP!

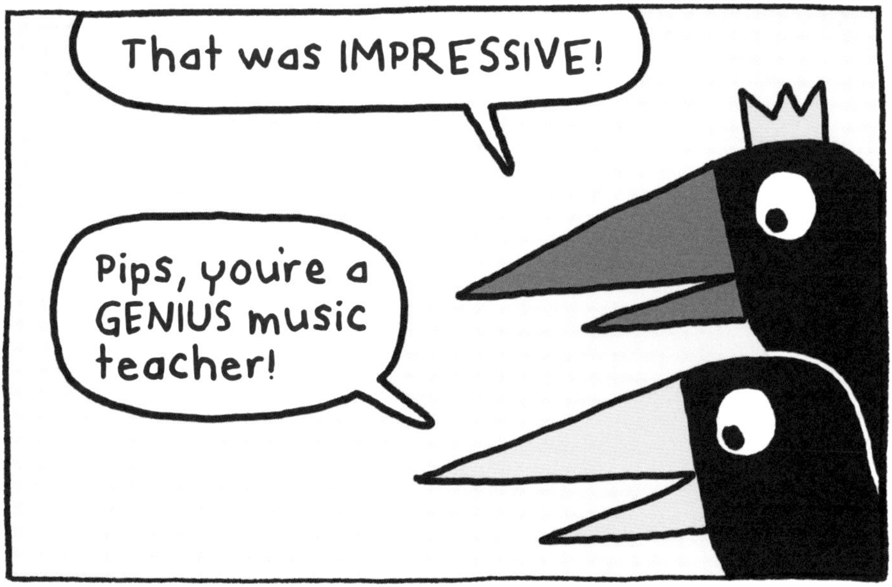
That was IMPRESSIVE!
Pips, youre a GENIUS music teacher!

Crows can imitate other birds' songs almost perfectly!

Everyone is tired. Time for bed!

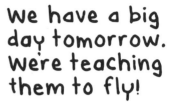

We have a big day tomorrow. We're teaching them to fly!

Oh, can I come?

Of course! Meet us here at dawn. The early bird gets the worm!

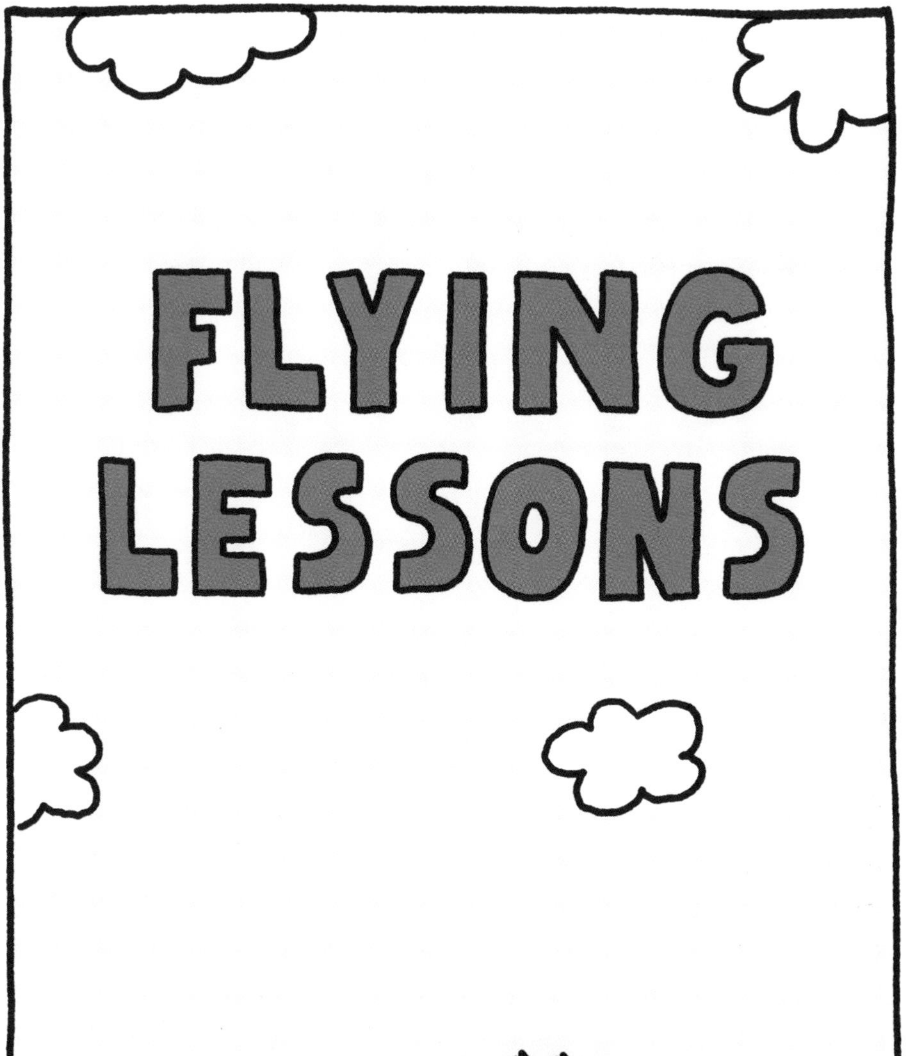
FLYING
LESSONS

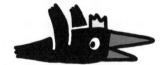

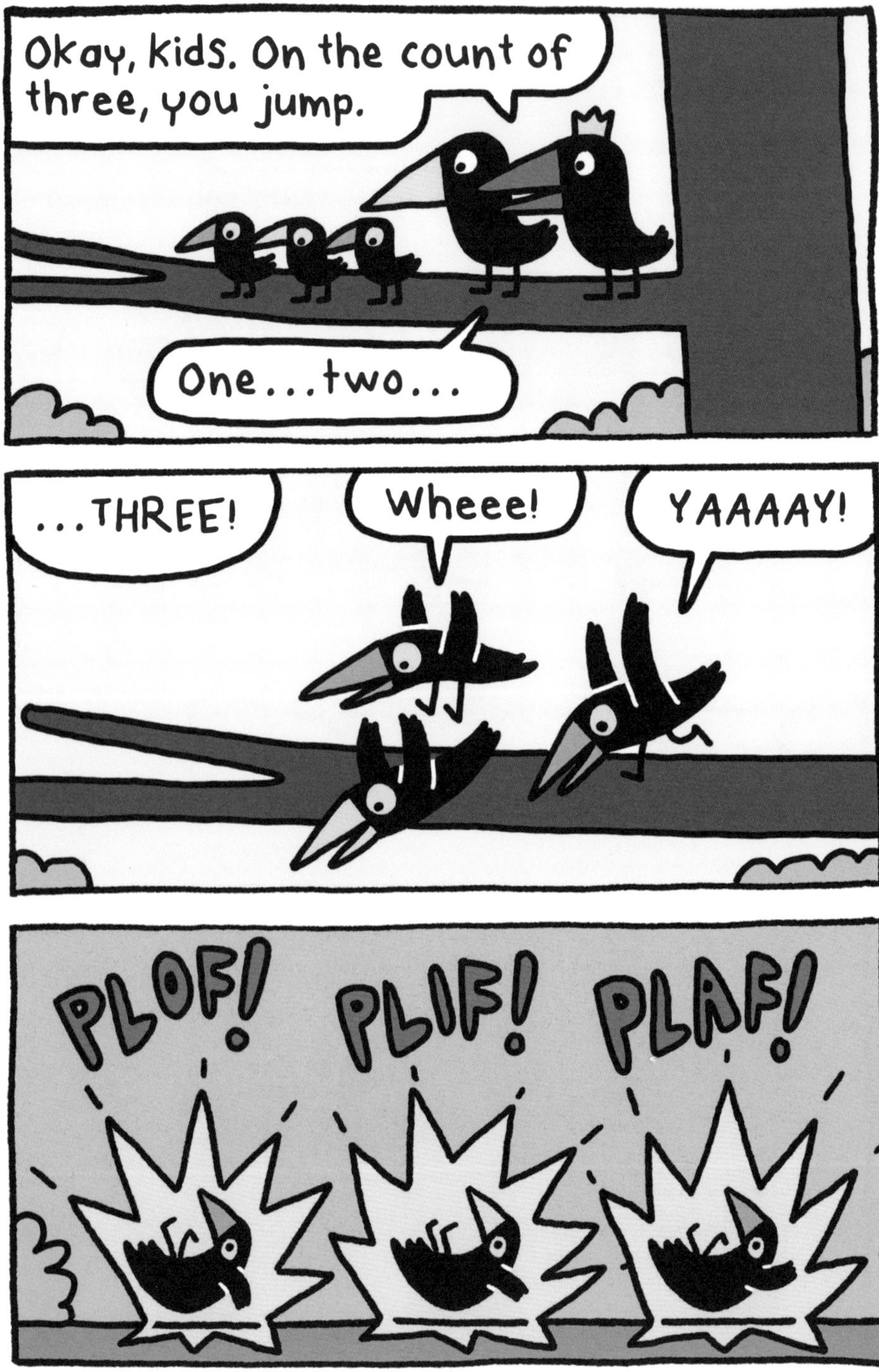

Okay, kids. On the count of three, you jump.
One...two...
...THREE!
Wheee!
YAAAAY!
PLOF!
PLIF!
PLAF!

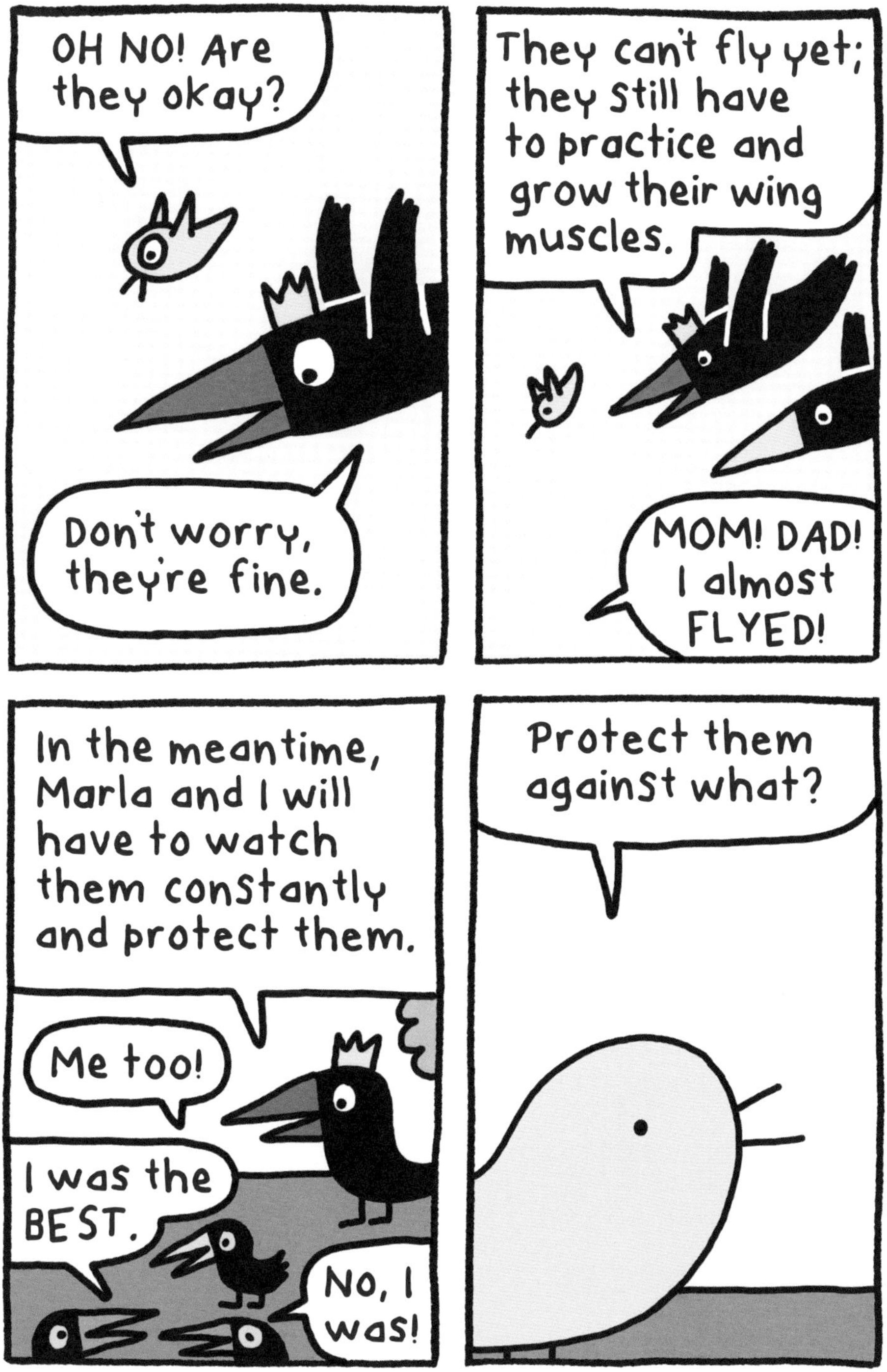
OH NO! Are they okay?
Don't worry, they're fine.
They can't fly yet; they still have to practice and grow their wing muscles.
MOM! DAD! I almost FLYED!
In the meantime, Marla and I will have to watch them constantly and protect them.
Me too!
I was the BEST.
No, I was!
Protect them against what?

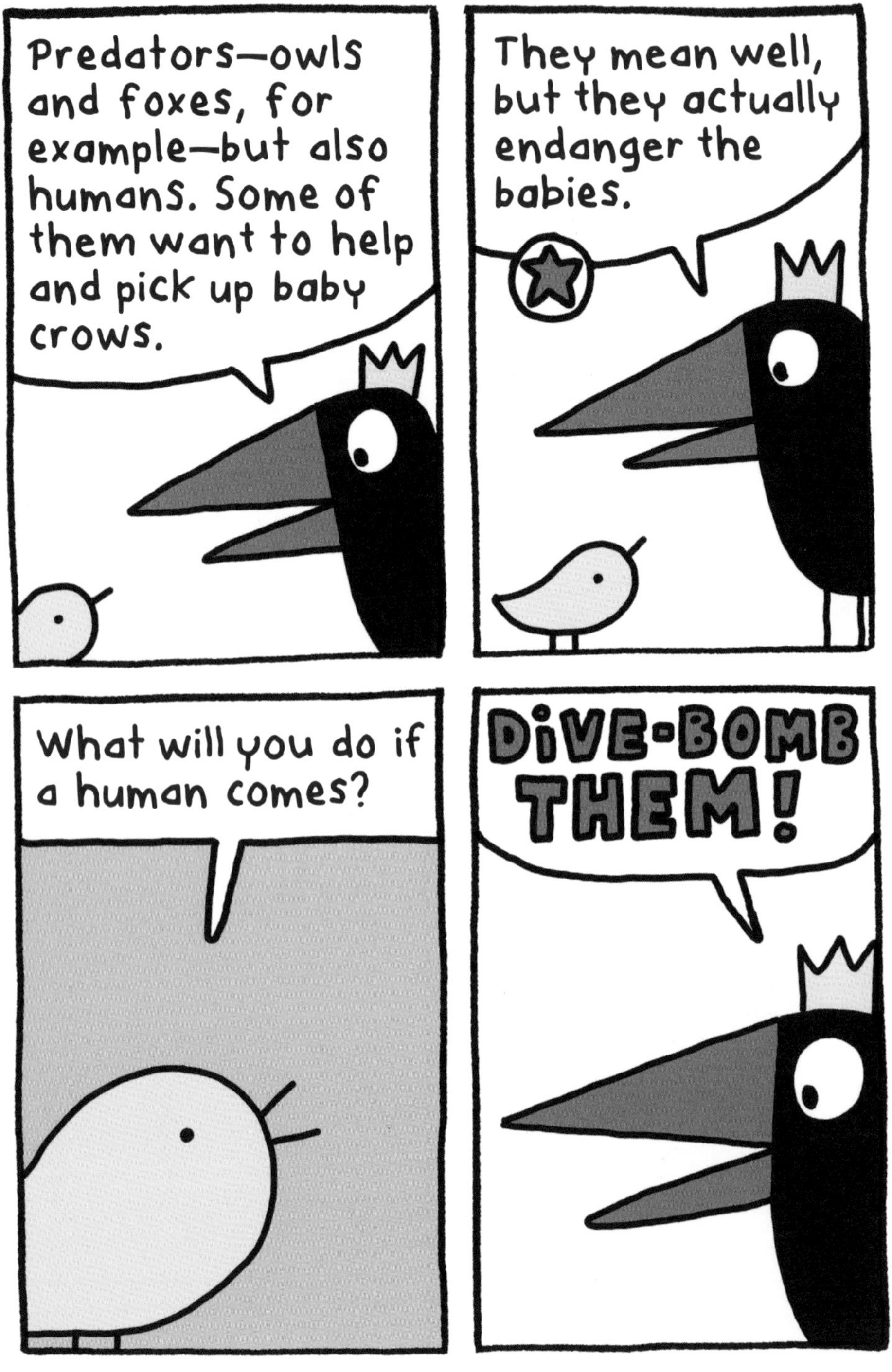

Predators—owls and foxes, for example—but also humans. Some of them want to help and pick up baby crows.
They mean well, but they actually endanger the babies.
What will you do if a human comes?
DIVE-BOMB THEM!

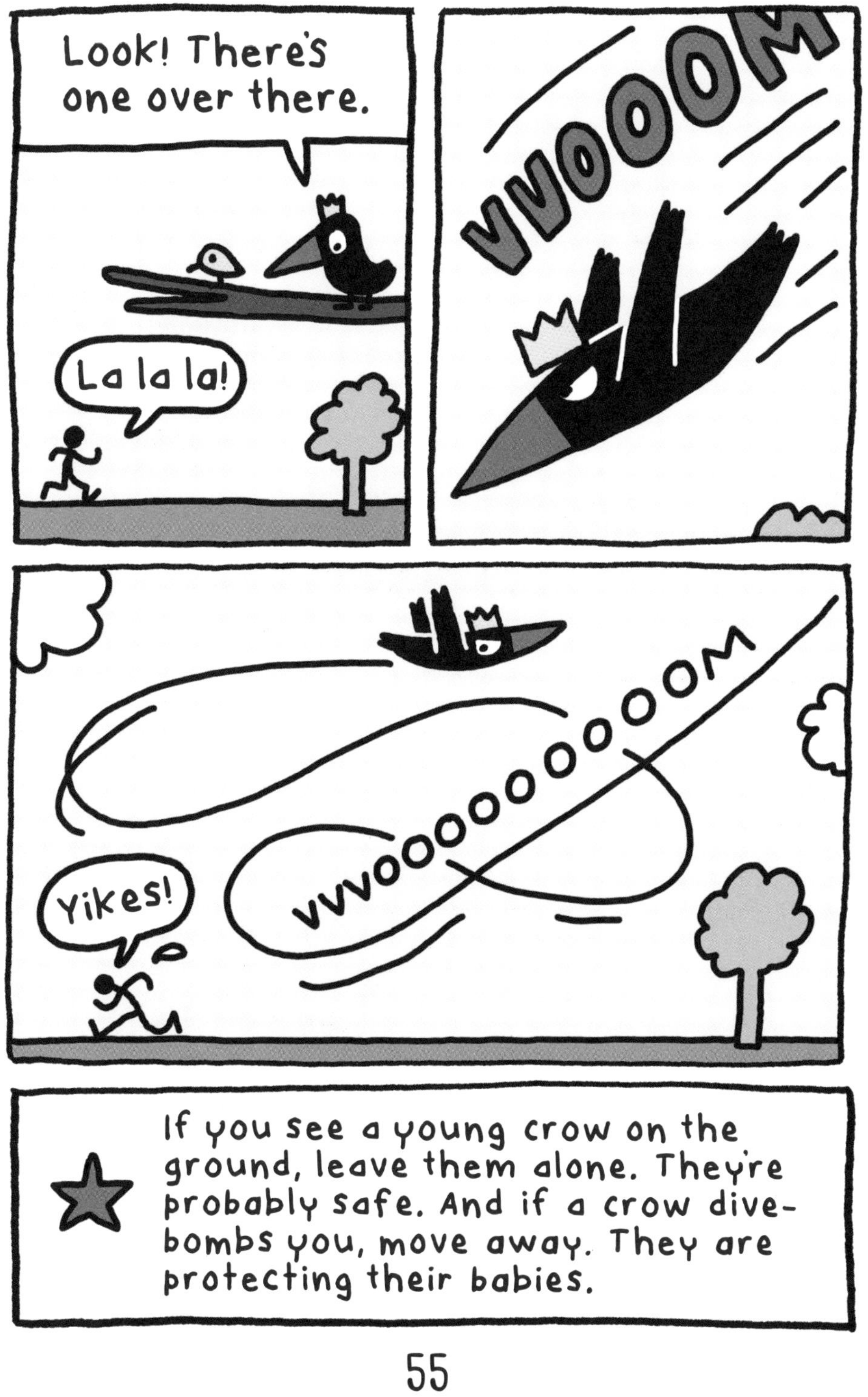
Look! There's one over there.
La la la!
VVOOOM
VVVOOOOOOOOOOOM
Yikes!

★ If you see a young crow on the ground, leave them alone. They're probably safe. And if a crow dive-bombs you, move away. They are protecting their babies.

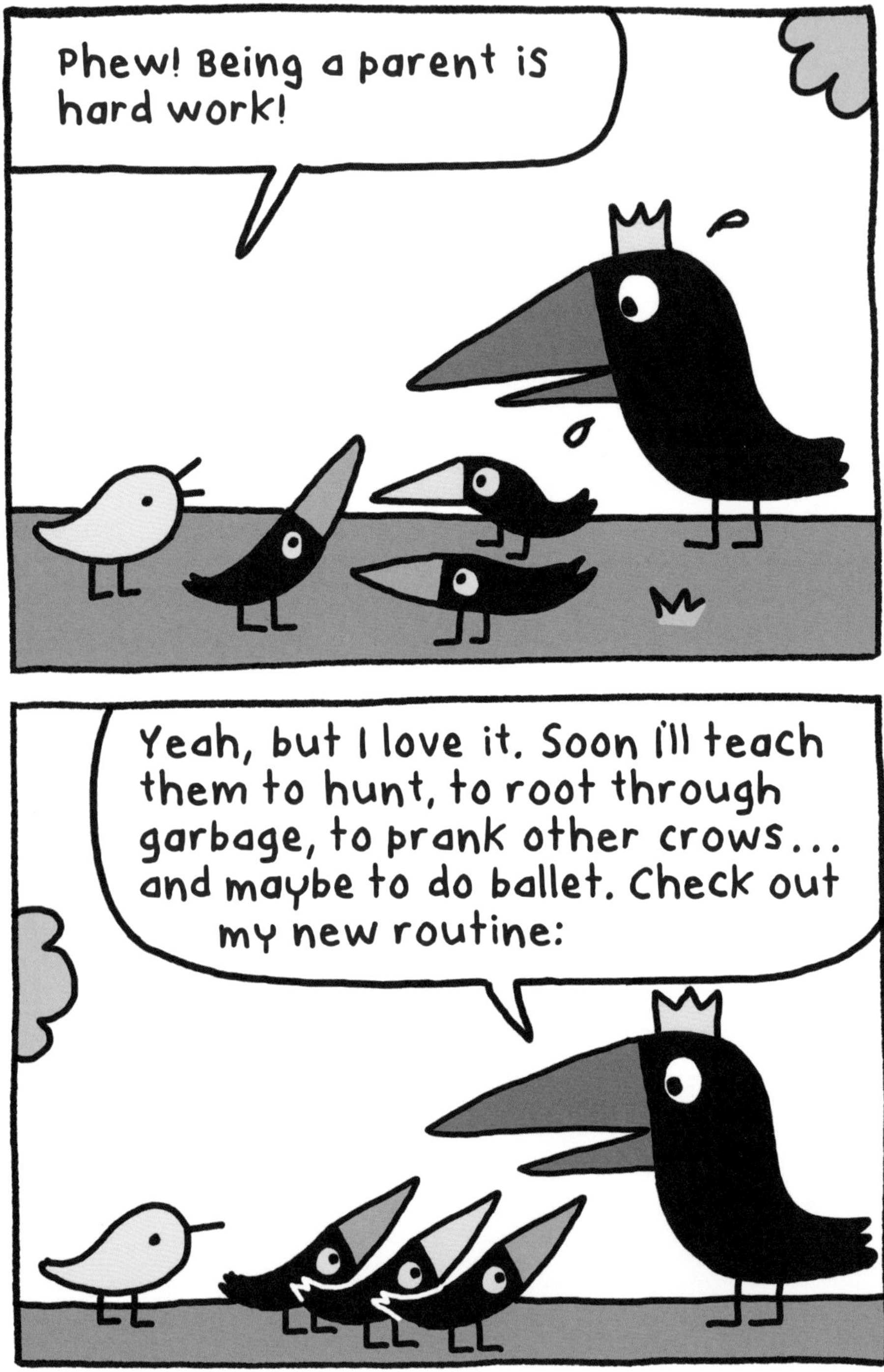
Phew! Being a parent is hard work!
Yeah, but I love it. Soon I'll teach them to hunt, to root through garbage, to prank other crows... and maybe to do ballet. Check out my new routine:

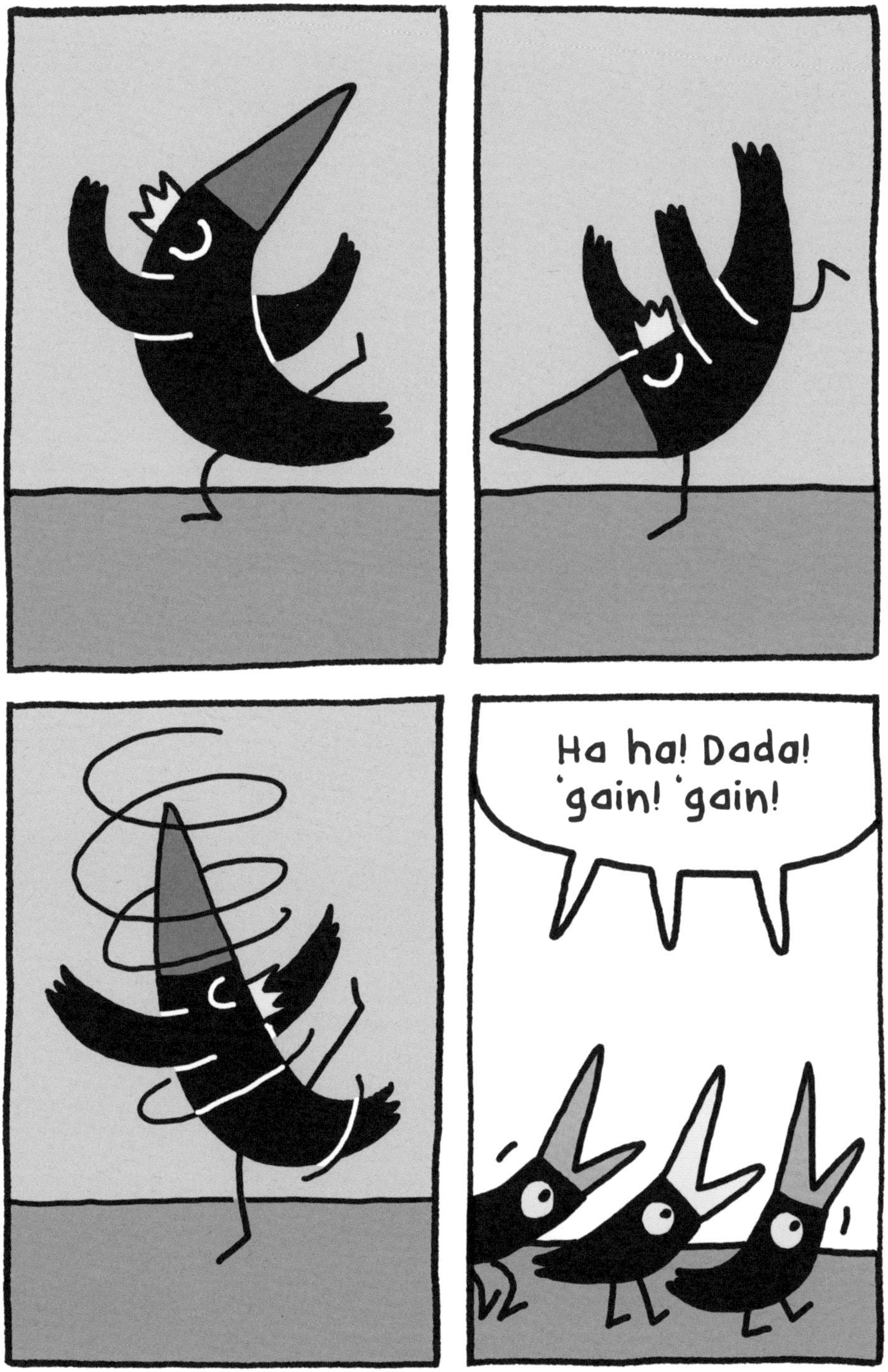
Ha ha! Dada! 'gain! 'gain!

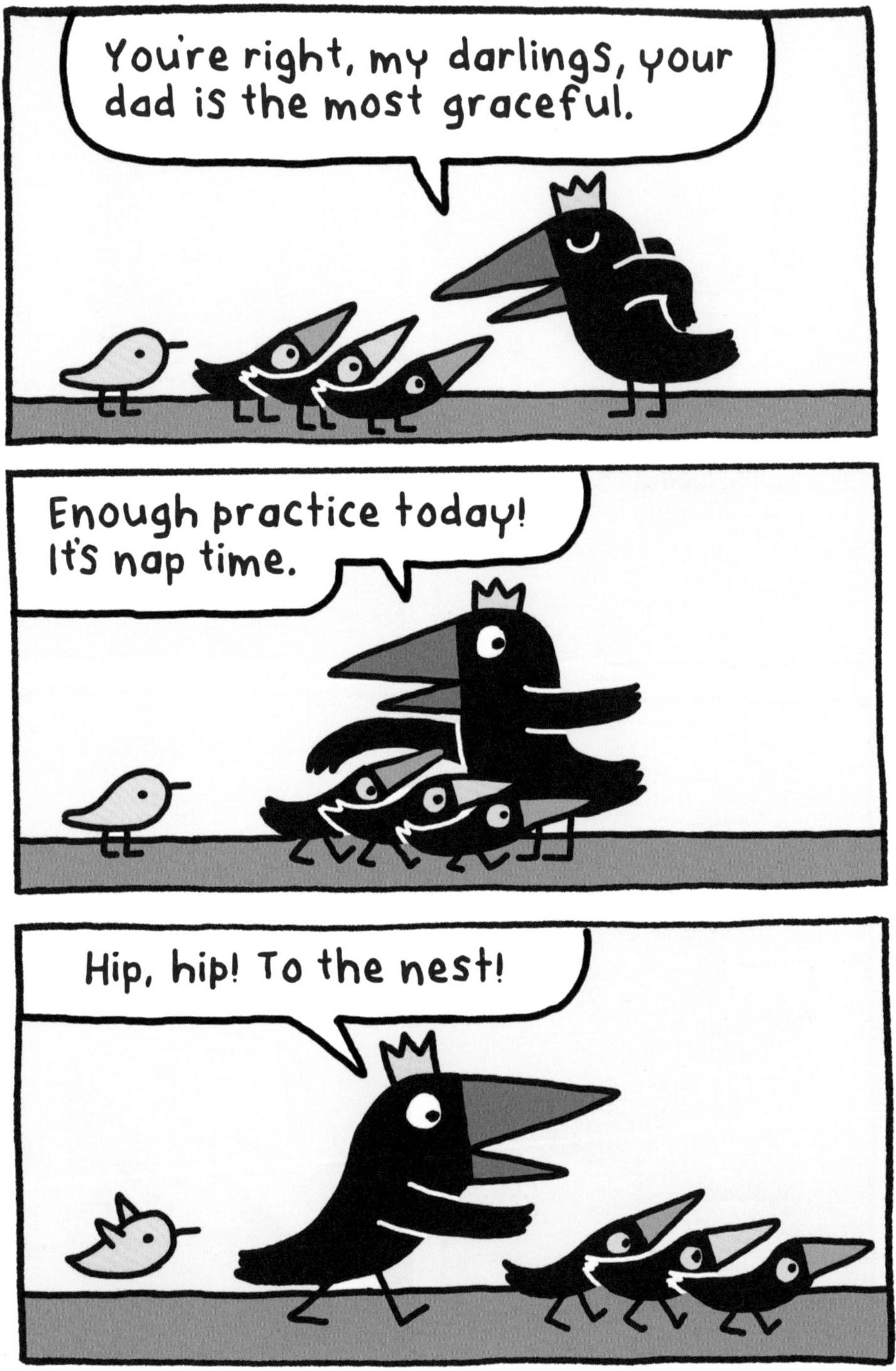
You're right, my darlings, your dad is the most graceful.
Enough practice today! It's nap time.
Hip, hip! To the nest!

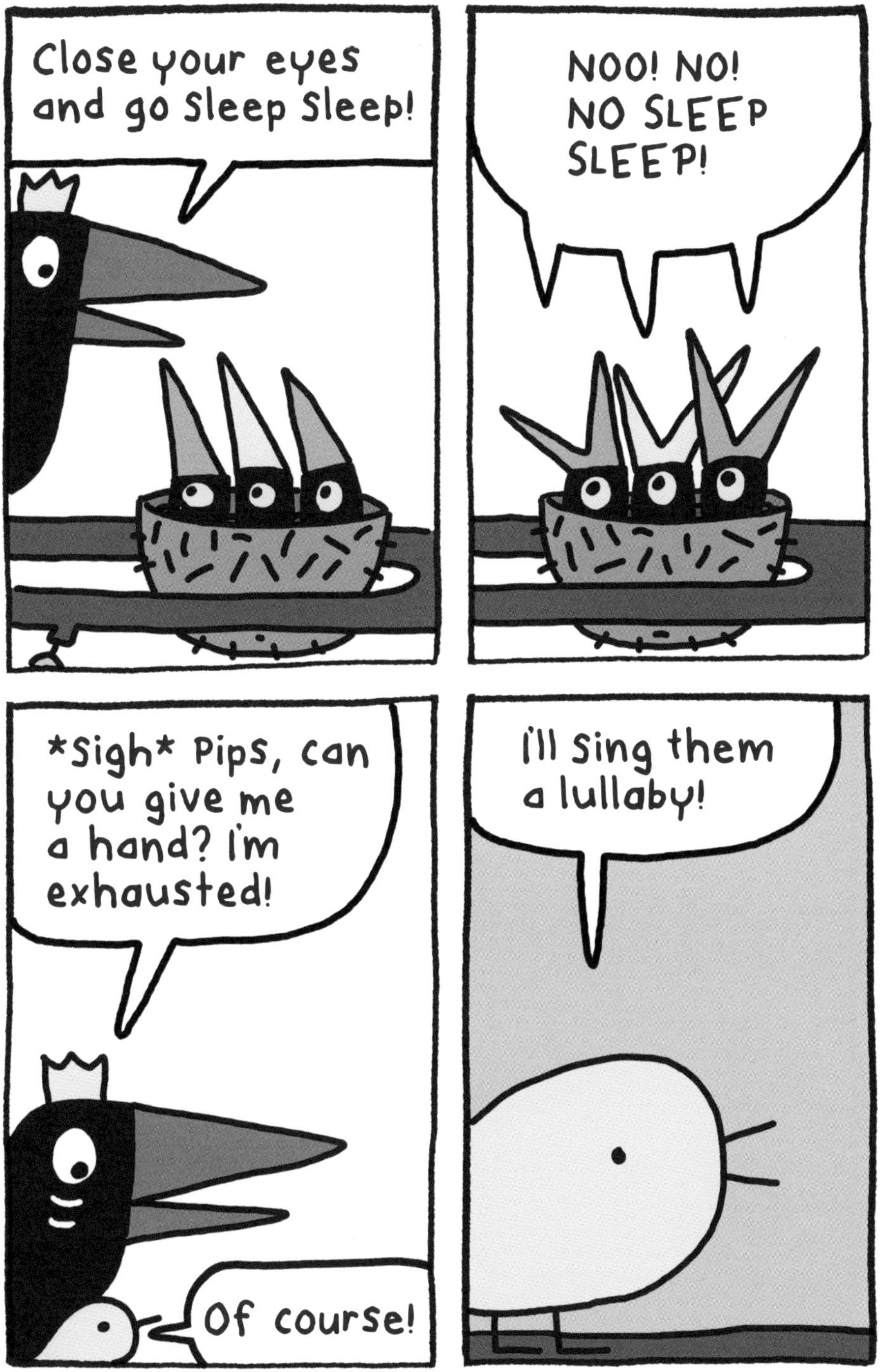
Close your eyes and go sleep sleep!
NOO! NO! NO SLEEP SLEEP!
Sigh Pips, can you give me a hand? I'm exhausted!
Of course!
I'll sing them a lullaby!

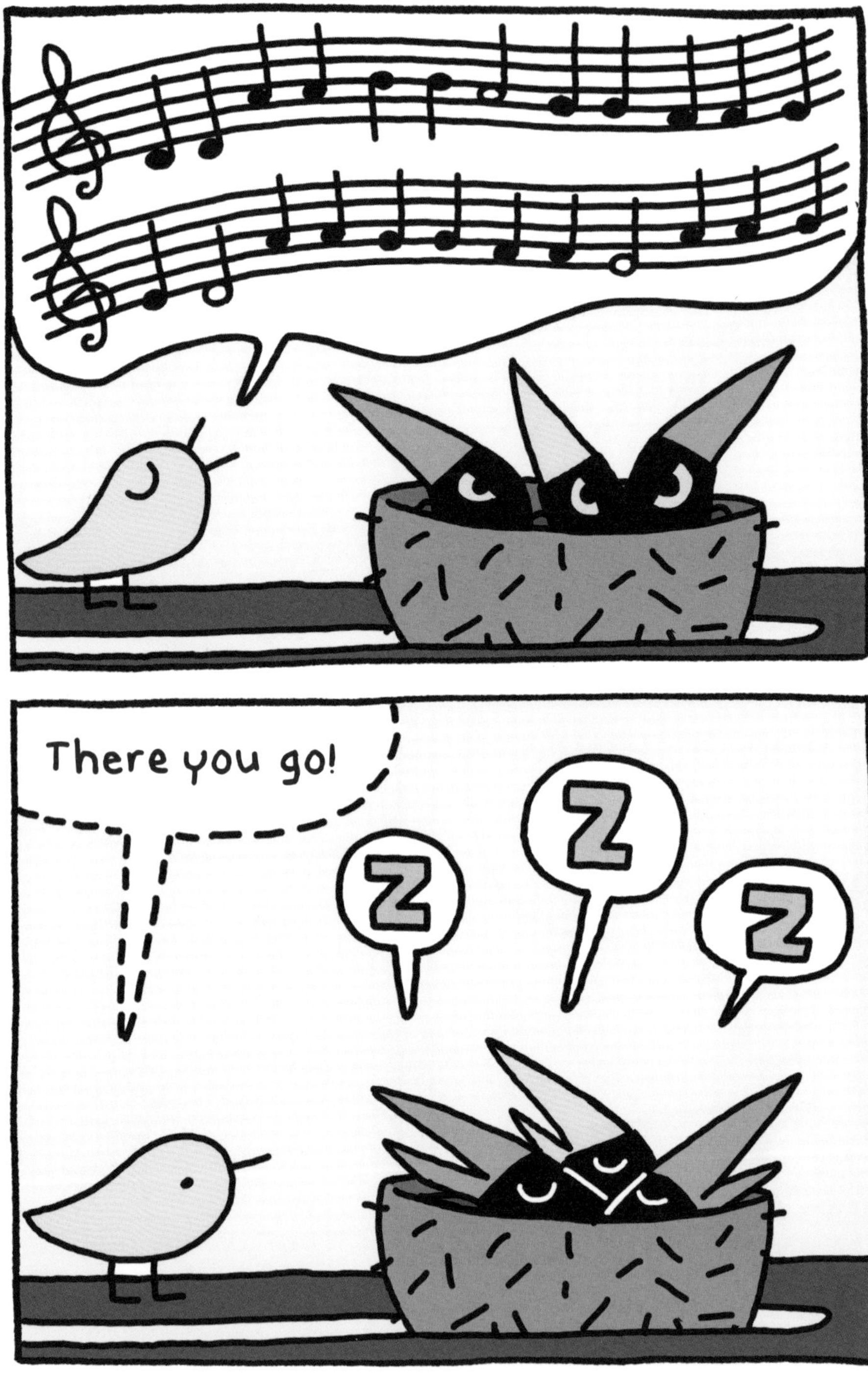
There you go!
Z
Z
Z

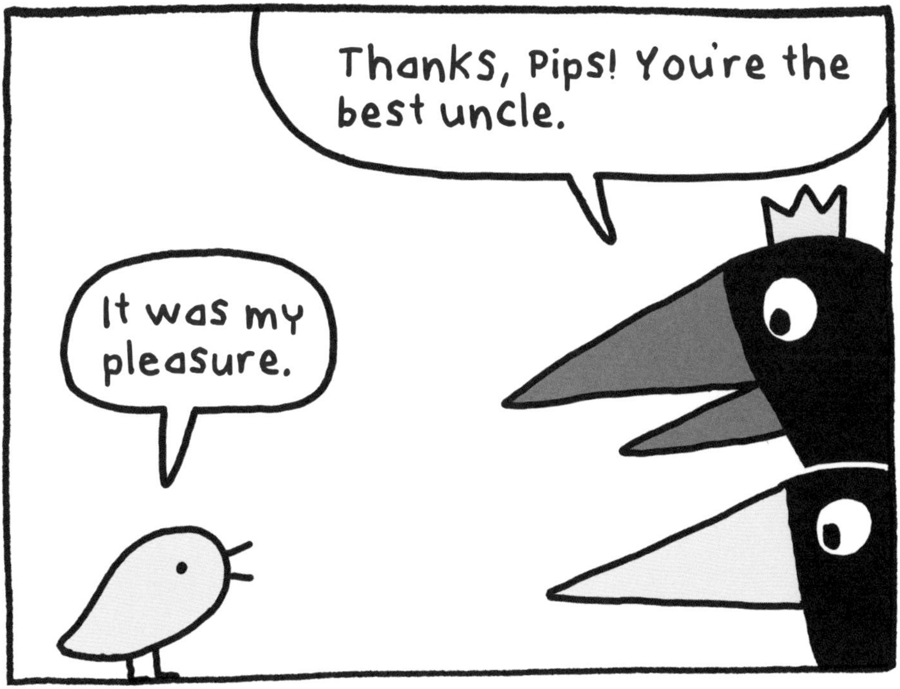
Thanks, Pips! You're the best uncle.
It was my pleasure.

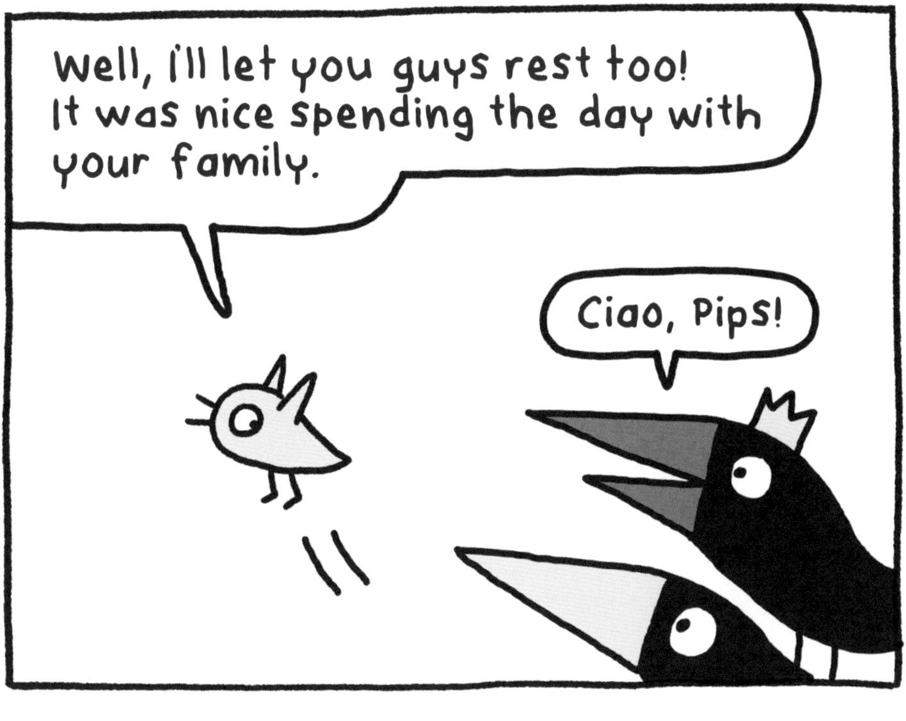
Well, I'll let you guys rest too! It was nice spending the day with your family.
Ciao, Pips!

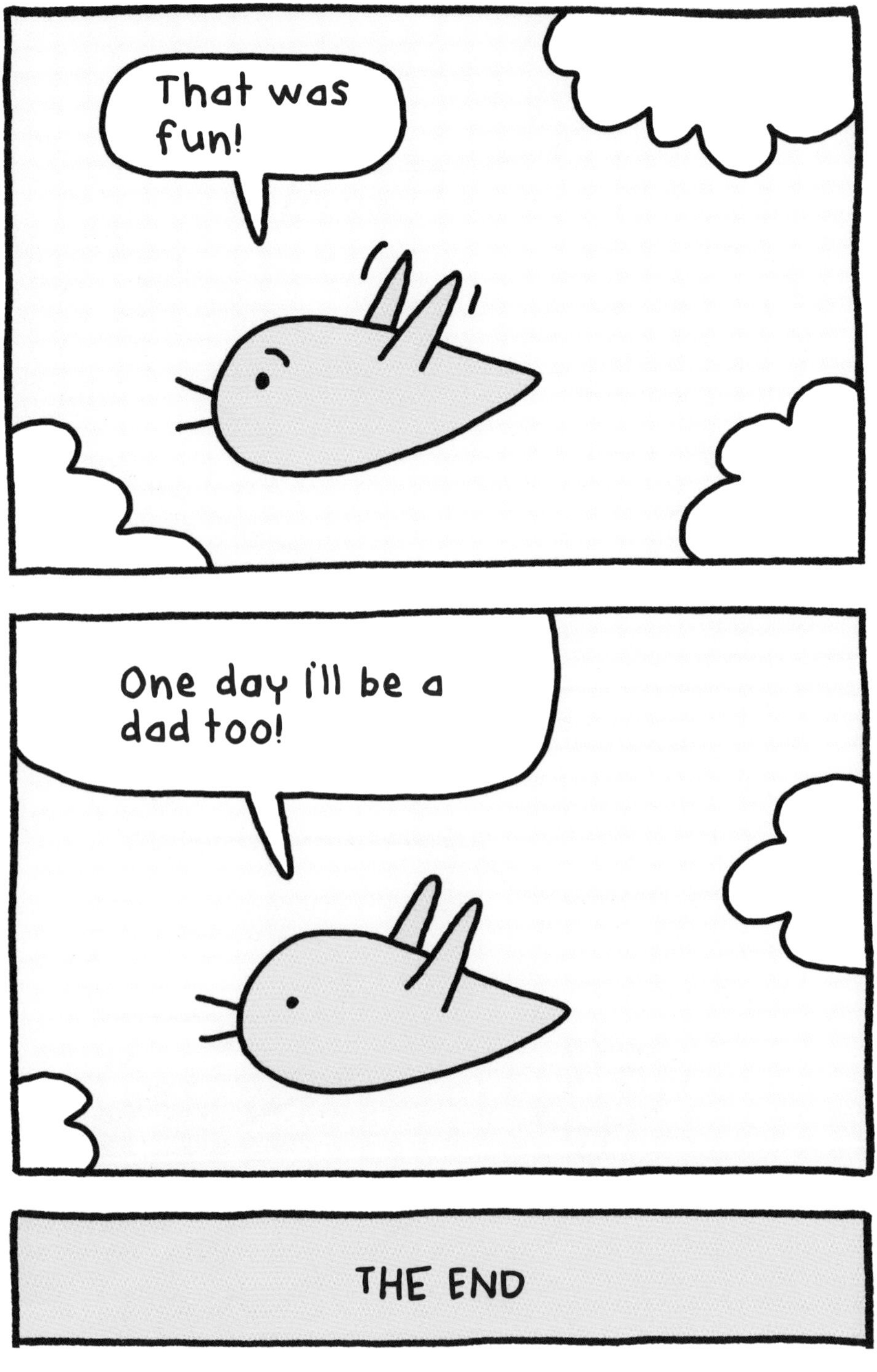
That was fun!
One day I'll be a dad too!
THE END

Note from the author:
While researching crows for this book, I found tons of cool facts that I didn't use. Here they are:

MORE CROW FACTS

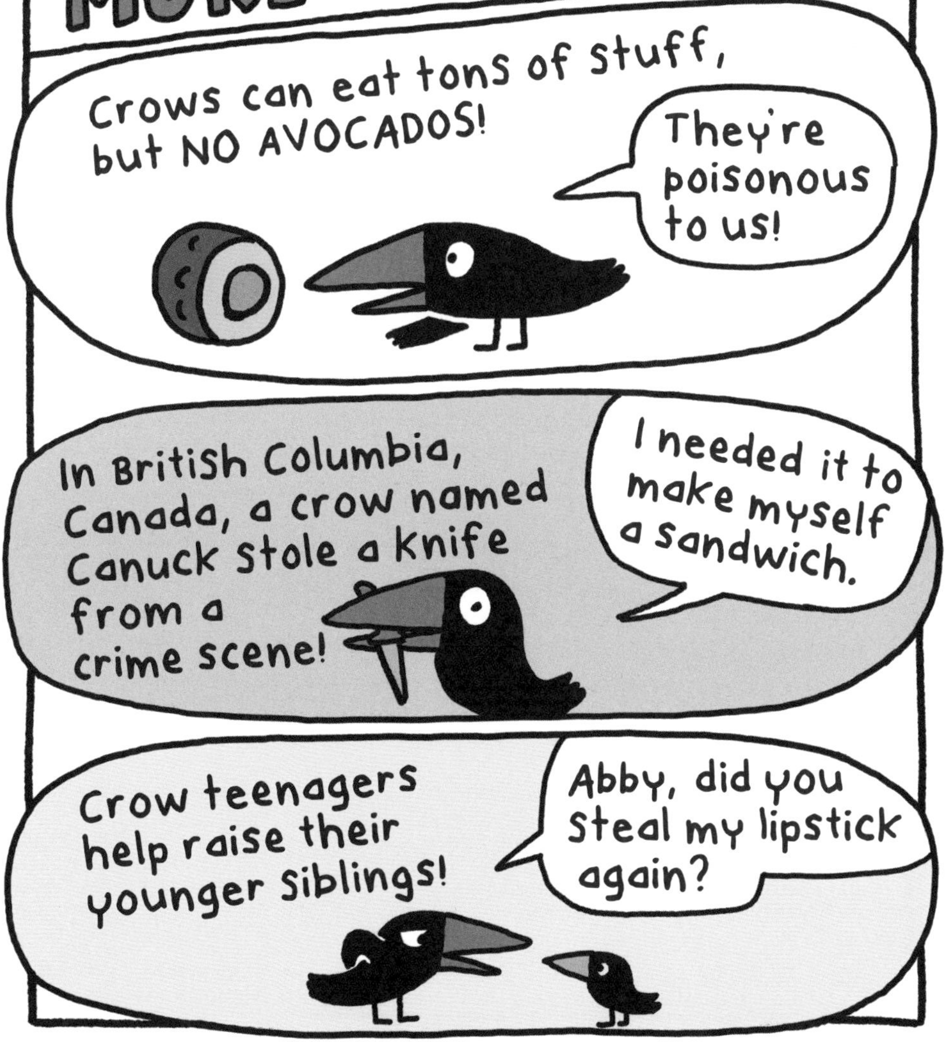

Crows can eat tons of stuff, but NO AVOCADOS!
They're poisonous to us!
In British Columbia, Canada, a crow named Canuck stole a knife from a crime scene!
I needed it to make myself a sandwich.
Crow teenagers help raise their younger siblings!
Abby, did you steal my lipstick again?

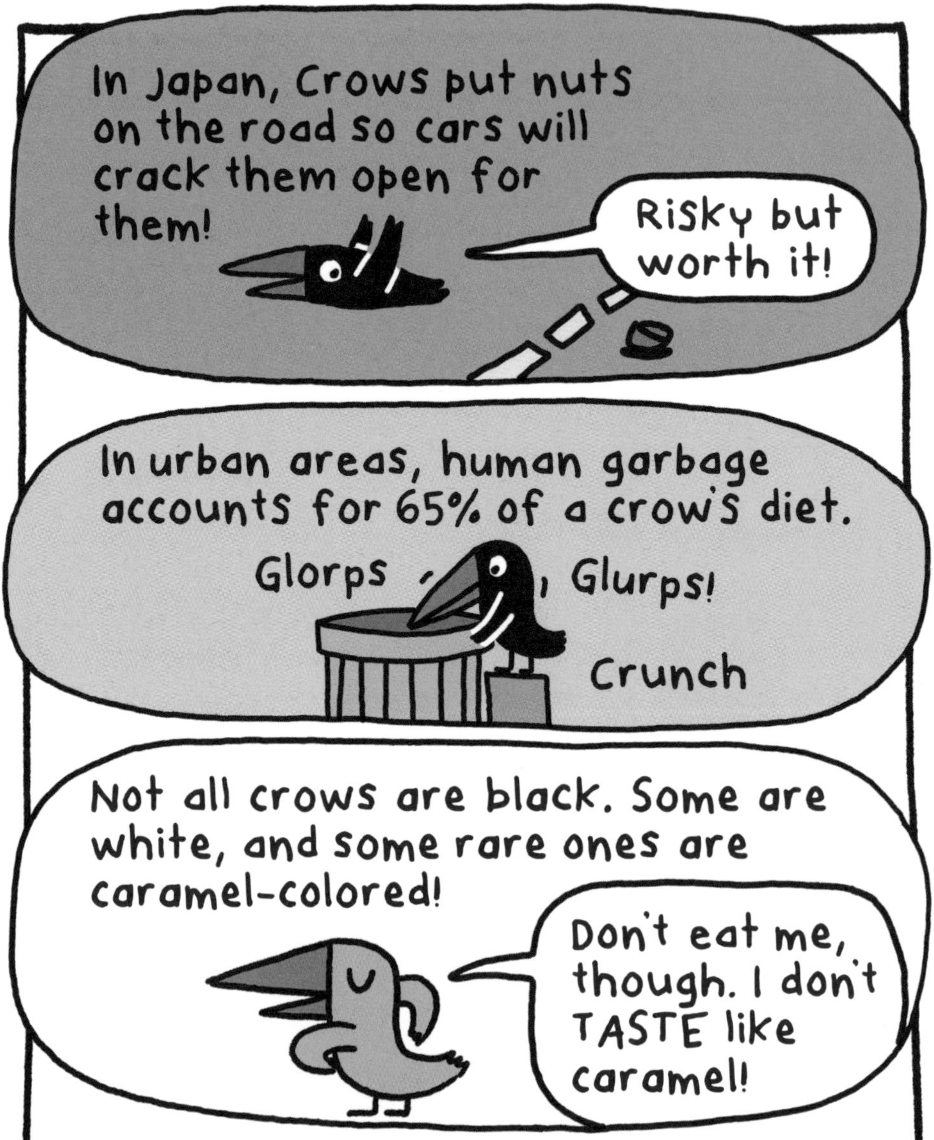
In Japan, Crows put nuts on the road so cars will crack them open for them!
Risky but worth it!
In urban areas, human garbage accounts for 65% of a crow's diet.
Glorps
Glurps!
Crunch
Not all crows are black. Some are white, and some rare ones are caramel-colored!
Don't eat me, though. I don't TASTE like caramel!

I hope that by now you like crows as much as I do! If you see one, say hi for me!

Elise Gravel

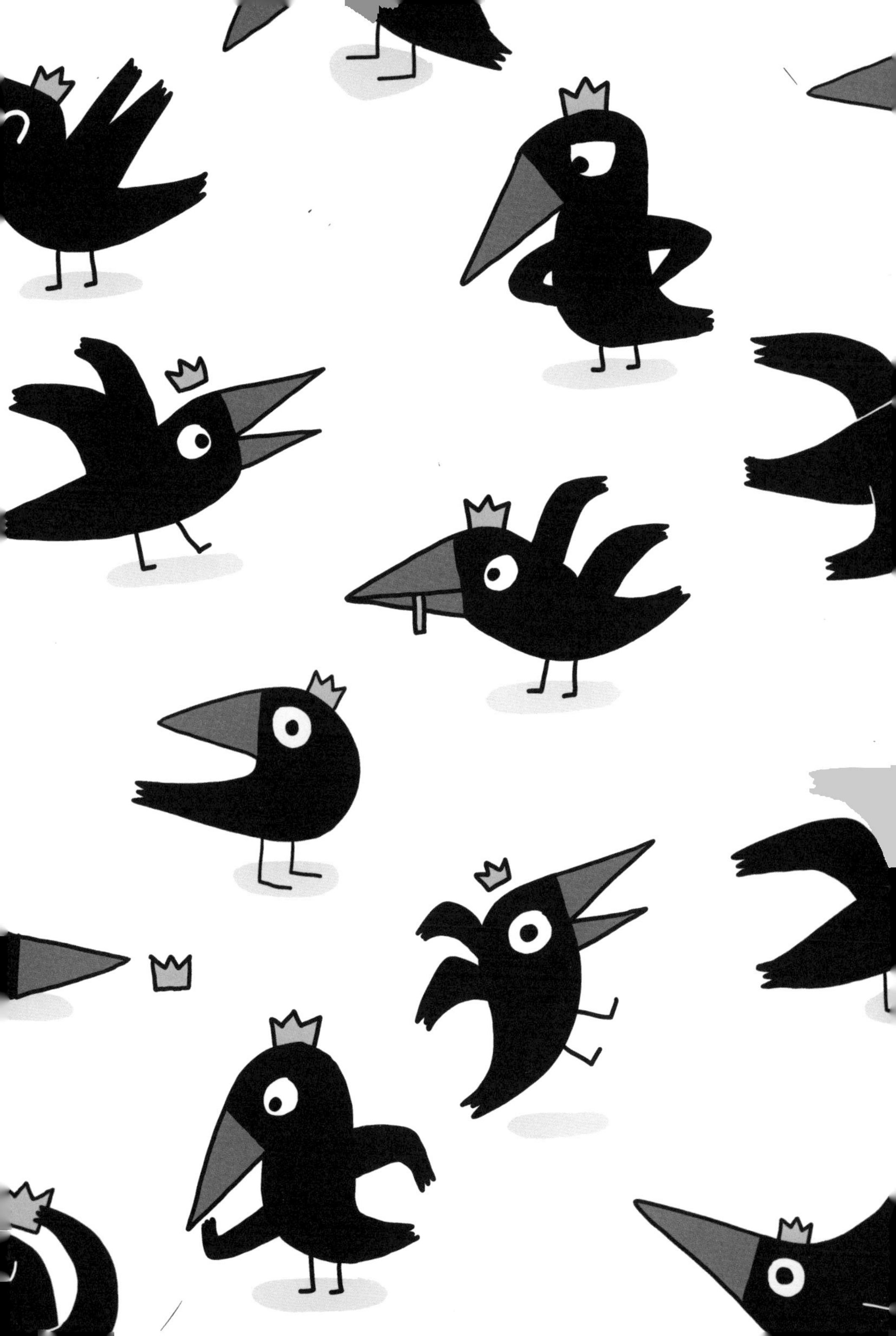

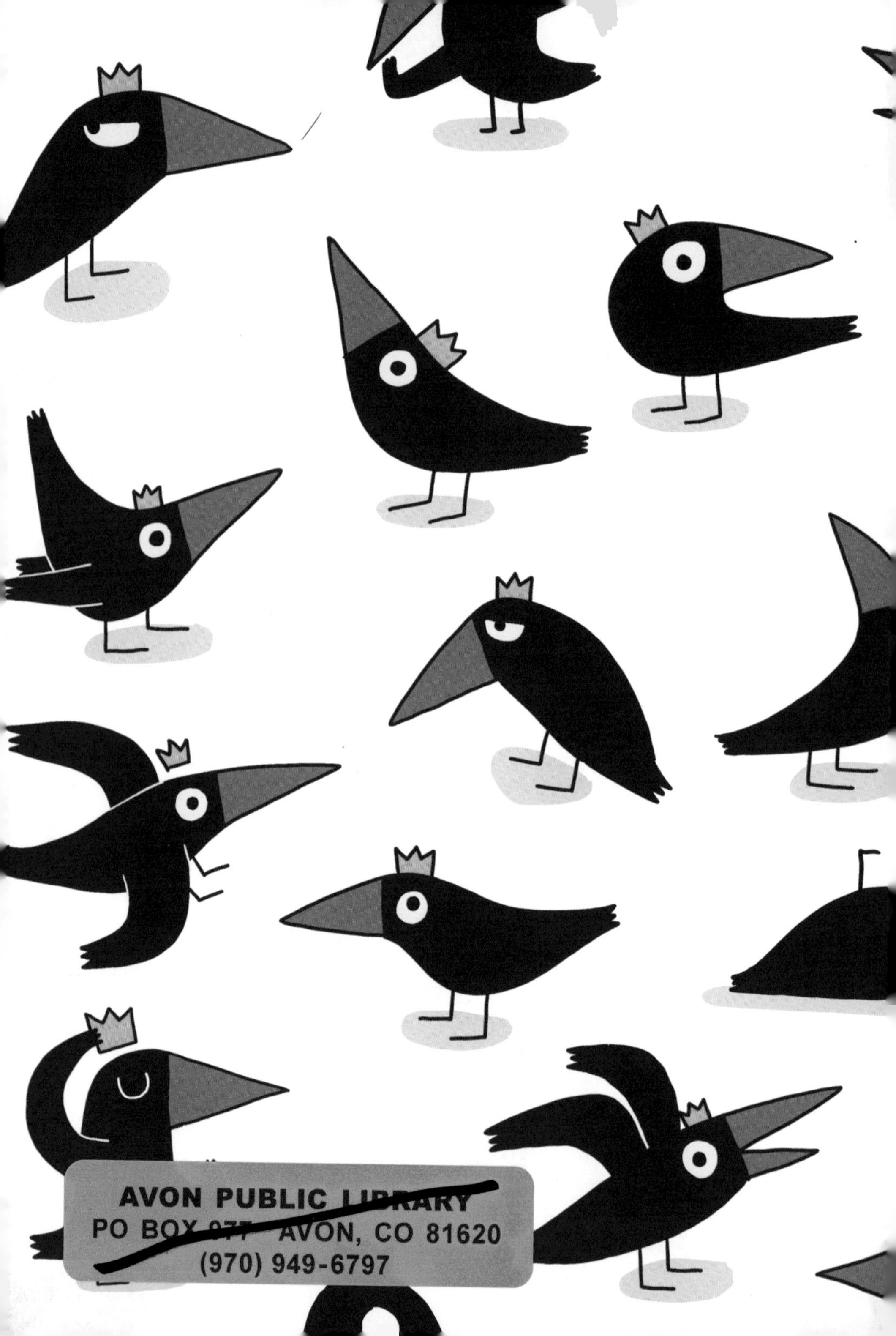